Prayer &
Pound Cake

THE BASS SISTERS' GUIDE TO SURVIVING
AND THRIVING IN BUSINESS

Dee Dee Bass Wilbon & Deana Bass Williams

Virginia

Prayer Works
&
Pound Cake Helps

Dee Dee
&
Deana

BondGirl Books

Published by BondGirl Books
www.bondgirlbooks.com
© 2021 BondGirl Books
Cover photo by XB Underwood
Designed by BondGirl Books
Unless otherwise stated, all Scripture citations are
from the New International Version.

ISBN: 9798787681864

This book may be purchased in bulk at special discounts for
sales promotion, corporate gifts, fundraising incentives,
houses of worship or educational purposes. For inquiries,
contact BondGirl Books at freebooks@bondgirlbooks.com.

To our Mama, our greatest cheerleader and prayer warrior.
Every day she shows us what it means to pray without ceasing.

And

To the memory of our Daddy, who taught us the importance of
loyalty and the value of hard work.

ACKNOWLEDGMENTS

We owe a debt of gratitude to a team of champions who worked to help us prepare this book for publication. Xavier Underwood is a jack of all trades and a master of many. The cover photography is because of his genius. Sharon Richmond is more than a makeup artist. She is a confidence booster, and we thank her for her in-studio magic. We are grateful for hairstylists who are always willing to fit us in their chairs. Kiarra Gilmore coiffed Dee Dee's crown on the cover. Deana's crown was coiffed by Tamecia Bradshaw. Last but certainly not least, to our first readers and long-serving champions also known as *The Wild Bunch*—Brian Wilbon, La Forrest Williams, Dorian Francis and Daylynn Francis—we say, "We love you and thank you!"

OUR STORY

There was a child went forth every day,
And the first object he looked upon and received with wonder or pity or
love or dread, that object he became,
And that object became part of him for the day or a certain part of the
day….or for many years or stretching cycles of years.

WALT WHITMAN

3

WHAT'S IN A NAME?

Prayer and Pound Cake

In March 2020, we were scheduled to host the first of what was to be a series of roundtables called Policy and Pound Cake at the National Press Club in Washington, D.C. The roundtables would bring together national communicators to discuss the best way to message complex policies. Well, you all know what happened in March of 2020. Courtesy of a global pandemic, we were stuck at home. We decided to turn Policy and Pound Cake into a weekly podcast. You can visit PolicyAndPoundCake.com to subscribe. The name Policy and Pound Cake came from the simple truth that the best conversations about policy take place at our mama's kitchen table with a massive slice of her homemade pound cake.

Even though we have been recording the lessons in this book for a decade, we did not settle on the title until about two months before our publication date. Every title fell flat. We hosted focus groups and collected surveys, and nothing seemed to work.

Then as if the fog cleared, the title *Prayer and Pound Cake* came to mind. Over the last 15 years, as we have grown our business, the two things that have been constants in our lives are prayers to our God in heaven and generous slices of our mama's homemade pound cake.

Mama's Prayers

L iving under the tutelage of a mother who understands the power of prayer and some mighty strong women who have prayed us into jobs and prayed us out of bad situations behooves us to examine the power of speaking to God.

Although we are unabashed Christians, we do not believe you must be a Christian to benefit from the wisdom that comes from the Bible. This book contains God-breathed Bible verses from which we derive business counsel. If we quoted anyone from Buddha to Socrates, the secular world would be comfortable accepting the lessons. You certainly do not have to be a Christian to benefit from the lessons and wise counsel of a host of women like our mama, whose daily conversations with God are nothing short of miracle-inducing.

We grew up seeing our mother speaking to God and speaking confidently about the things that God promised in his word. She continues to declare the promises of God on our lives and our world. There is no trial or valley that we experienced that was bigger than our mama's God. Her life teaches us that the power of prayer is more than rubbing a genie lamp. Our mama has an intimate relationship with Christ. This daily relationship gives her confidence that every single thing that we do to bring honor to God will work out in the end. The prayers of a righteous mama are powerful and effective.

Mama's Pound Cake

B efore you ask, no, we will never share the top-secret recipe. We don't even know it. Two people on earth know it, Mama and Dee Dee's daughter, Daylynn.

Our mama's pound cake is heaven on earth and legendary in our circles. It is the gift she brings to family and friends for all occasions of delight and sorrow. Over the last 15 years as we have grown our business, it oddly represents peace on earth. For us, Mama's pound cake means comfort in times of trouble and joy in times of celebration.

Stay tuned...We can feel a Pound Cake Series of books in the works.

GROWING UP BASS

Daddy, Mama and Hard Work

We grew up in Columbus, Georgia, a town on the state's western border. Our parents were by no stretch of anyone's imagination rich. But our very working-class neighborhood of blue-collar and white-collar families could hardly be described as poor.

Our family and neighbors lived on the brink of and beyond paycheck to paycheck. Unfortunately, the discipline of saving, investing, and living well below your means to get ahead had not been passed down from our grandparents to our parents. However, our daddy and mama did inherit a work ethic that said no job was too dirty if it meant providing for their family. Therefore, we grew up seeing two parents unafraid of putting their shoulder to the plow and working.

Our daddy did not have the advantage of a high school diploma. He provided for us by laboring as a drywall construction worker—the work that his father and older brothers had done before him. Throughout Georgia, our daddy and his twin brother, our Uncle James, were among the most sought after in the business.

We participated in *take your daughter to work day* long before it was fashionable. The tasks that Daddy gave us were not difficult. We cleaned up job sites by picking up trash, nails, and broken pieces of drywall. Being on the job gave us an appreciation for how difficult construction work is. Drywall construction is not for the lazy or idle. It is backbreaking. Under the heat of a Georgia summer sun, it could be brutal and dangerous.

When politicians and pundits with little experience in anything other than talking say Americans will not take jobs requiring true sweat, we say *rubbish*. Our daddy did. Many fathers and mothers would.

Our daddy's experience as a drywall construction worker without a high school education framed our view of business. We knew Daddy was great at his job. But he did not control the game. David Olsen owned the construction company, and he controlled the game.

David was an honest family man, God-fearing, and patriotic. His generosity spilled over to our entire family. He and Dee Dee share a birthday, and she was often the benefactor of extra gifts. We do not doubt that David himself would put shoulder to the plow to do the grueling work to support his wife and boys. But he did not have to do the grueling work. Our daddy did it for him. Our Uncle James and many other men did the hard manual labor for him. While David paid well, he kept the lion's share of every contract. We say that without resentment. David's name was on the door. Entrepreneurship works that way. To the owner go the spoils.

We were young when our daddy worked for David, but the lessons of ownership always remained with us. David earned our daddy's loyalty by paying him good wages, showing kindness to his little girls, and paying respect to his bride. David was as loyal as he could be to Daddy. But when construction costs and illegal immigration began to rise, David had to look out for his family by looking out for his business. Ownership allows you to make these decisions.

We learned equally essential lessons about education, business and ownership from our mama. Mama attended Morris Brown College in Atlanta and completed her degree at Columbus College (now Columbus State University). The responsibilities of being a new wife and mother slowed her down. But she could not be stopped. Mama's professional pursuits reinforced the idea of hard work.

Mama began her career as a schoolteacher. The work schedule was perfect for the mother of two school-aged children. But even as she worked her day job, she always had an idea for side ventures to bring extra cash to the family coffers. She cultivated bright ideas on the verge of bloom. They were never unrealistic or unattainable endeavors. They were usually creative services. The most memorable was painting street addresses on the curb in front of homes. For a reasonable fee, Mama would use stencils to paint your street address. Your visitors would never miss your home. Other side hustles of Mama's included 3D Cleaning Services and 3D Resume Writing.

Most people do not have the stomach for entrepreneurship, even if they have a heart for entrepreneurship. However, our childhood experiences watching our daddy and mama confirmed that we had both the stomach and heart. We knew starting our own business would not happen overnight, but business ownership was the only professional pursuit that excited us.

Formal and Informal Education

In the mid-1980s, we were plucked from our public schools and transferred to private schools. Our classmates changed from working-class children to the children of the people who hired the working class. Dee Dee moved to Pacelli, a Catholic school attracting middle-class protestants. Deana transferred to Brookstone, a private school on the northern border of the city.

Dee Dee transferred to Pacelli because Daddy happened to visit the public school where she was enrolled. We say, "happened to visit" because as much as he adored us, Daddy left everything related to school to Mama. However, on this particular day, Mama's schedule shifted the task of dropping off or picking up to Daddy. Whatever he saw was enough for him to tell Mama in no uncertain terms that Dee Dee was transferring.

He did not seem concerned that the school year had just started, and Dee Dee had earned a coveted spot on the junior varsity cheerleading squad, or that the school was within walking distance to our home and did not require navigating carpools.

Within a week, Mama enrolled Dee Dee at Pacelli. Dee Dee was faced with kids unlike any she had experienced. She was among bourgeois black students who summered at Martha's Vineyard. She was among white military brats who had seen much of the country and the world.

Dee Dee did not skip a beat. Gregarious and friendly, her larger-than-life personality helped earn her a spot on the cheering squad. She also quickly became a member of the modeling teen board for Gayfers, a local department store, where she was a celebrated mannequin model and part-time gift wrapper.

If Dee Dee's departure from public school was because she was too much of a social butterfly, Deana's departure from public school was because she was a bit of a social misfit. Mama wisely reasoned that her quirky little girl would be less of an oddball in private school. Deana also did not need to follow in Dee Dee's popular footsteps.

Pacelli and Brookstone, without argument, were the two best high schools in our city. They were among the most academically challenging schools in the entire state. We did not know it at the time, but academic training was a secondary benefit to attending Pacelli and Brookstone. The primary benefit was first-hand exposure to the one-percenters who, as adults, would take the reins of leadership from their fathers and control the wealth of this nation.

Working Girls

After graduating from college, Dee Dee immediately landed a job with MBNA America Bank in Wilmington, Delaware. Before being bought by Bank of America, MBNA was the largest issuer of credit cards in North America.

Working at MBNA gave Dee Dee a close-up view of corporate America and the one-percenters who ran it. For what it's worth, at MBNA, Dee Dee witnessed that the self-reinforcing loop of success did not practice racism as much as it did nepotism. Ascension to the c-suite relied heavily on being granted access to the inner circle. The one-percenters who controlled that space naturally invited their friends and family. If your friends and family lack melanin and you are in charge of populating the c-suite, the c-suite will also lack melanin.

In 2002, a congressman from California, U.S. Rep. Howard P. "Buck" McKeon offered Deana a job as his press secretary. The decision was easy. Living in Washington, D.C. placed Deana less than three hours from Dee Dee and her brand new baby nephew. Moreover, Deana's job on Capitol Hill allowed both Dee Dee and Deana to witness some of the most influential people on the planet in action.

The strategies and prayers shared in this book are informed by our life in a working-class family being educated among and working alongside the one-percent.

THIRTY-ONE DAYS OF CONSCIOUS CHOICE AND DISCIPLINED PRAYER

We have had the great honor of getting to know Dr. Ben Carson over the past few years. His 2016 presidential campaign hired Bass Public Affairs. We have heard the world-renowned neurosurgeon turned cabinet secretary say countless times, "The person who has the most to do with you and what happens to you in life is you." We take Dr. Carson's wise counsel to heart. We did not grow up with the pedigree or privileges of most of our classmates, but we have within our power the ability to read and learn, and work and achieve success.

Jim Collins, author of *Good to Great,* speaks and writes about conscious choice and discipline. Greatness is not essentially a function of circumstance. Collins says, "Greatness, it turns out, is primarily a matter of conscious choice and discipline."

Have you ever made the conscious choice to spend 31 days praying for your business?

We are not social scientists or academics. Our business experience comes from dreaming about starting a business, praying about starting a business, and, starting a business. We are sisters, business partners and huge fans of anyone who takes the leap and enters a product or service into the marketplace. Understanding from personal experience what it is like to be on the verge of starting a business and even closing a business, we offer this book as an opportunity to do what Christian business owners rarely take time to do, stop and pray for their business.

This book is our way of encouraging you to spend a month, 31 deliberate days, pouring powerful prayers directly into your business. So, whether you choose to stop and slowdown in the wee small hours of the morning, midday or midnight, we are excited that you are taking time to pray.

We know that praying strategically to Jesus the Christ will change your life. We also know that the Scriptures in this book are powerful and God-breathed. We hope the lessons based on our 15 years of running a healthy business will bless you.

OWNING AND GROWING YOUR AWESOMENESS

In case you have not been adequately informed, please consider this official notification that you are awesome.

UNKNOWN

DAY 1 - THE DIAMONDS ARE REAL

Our first lesson comes from a young entrepreneur who has governed his actions for as long as we have known him with clarity, courage and competence. To this day, Nathan Imperiale remains a dear and trusted friend. Deana met Nathan when she worked as Director of Coalitions for the House Conference under Chairman Deborah Pryce. Most members of Congress supported their leadership's charge to increase diversity in congressional offices. Today there is an official House Office of Diversity. For a brief spell 20 years ago, for the House Conference, it was Deana with no budget.

She did have the freedom to hire a non-paid intern. Nathan entered our lives. At the time, Nathan was a 19-year-old kid from The George Washington University. Years later, he confessed to Deana that he wanted to quit in his first week. He found Deana a bit crazy.

Nathan probably still thinks that Deana (and Dee Dee for that matter) is a little nuts. Praying women do look, sound and behave in ways that appear crazy at times. They can see a hopeful reality that others simply do not see. As the world crumbles around you, when you have stored up a lifetime of direct conversations with the King of the Universe, you may look insane to the world.

Fortunately for Deana and the House Conference, the young intern did not jump ship. Instead, Nathan hung around, and by thinking like a true one-percenter, he was paid staff at the House Conference before he graduated. After graduation, he started his own media firm, leaving with the House Conference as one of his first major contracts.

Today, his digital marketing firm, NJI Media, is wildly successful with offices in Virginia, London and Singapore. Nathan is wicked smart, exceedingly kind and extremely capable. His success springs largely from how he was taught to think and behave from the day he drew his first breath.

An example of the fundamentally different way Nathan approaches life and the way we once approached life came in a tiny jewelry box that Deana brought into her office on Capitol Hill. Mama sent a dragonfly necklace, knowing Deana's love for dragonflies long before it became the Bass Public Affairs logo.

Deana wore the necklace to work and showed it to Nathan. He marveled over it in such a way that Deana had to confess, "You know these are cubic zirconia!"

Nathan looked shocked and said, "Wow! Really?"

She gave him the crazy side-eye and sighed, "Yes," while thinking, "He actually believes my mama sent me a diamond dragonfly necklace."

More than three years later, when Deana and Nathan had long left Capitol Hill, she was home in Georgia for a visit. Wearing the lovely dragonfly necklace, Deana recalled the story and shared it with Mama, only to learn that the diamonds are real.

Nathan's reality is grounded in believing he deserves real diamonds. Why would anyone send him anything less? This way of thinking governs every deal that our poster child one-percenters make. Whether they act intentionally or unintentionally, how they approach big and small decisions leads to significant wins. Their fundamental belief is that they deserve the very best and govern their actions accordingly.

It is critical to point out that we in no way fault or blame those born into the one-percent for having this fundamentally optimistic and self-confident worldview. On the contrary, we admire this way of thinking. As soon as we identified it, we tried to adopt it in our own lives. When our attitude is bent towards winning, we typically do. In many ways, this is fighting against our natural self.

If we believe what the Lord's word says about us, it will be easy to approach every obstacle with a victorious attitude. God's word says we are fearfully and wonderfully made. He took special care to knit every aspect of our character while we were in our mother's womb. If the King of the Universe feels this way about us, it should be easy to approach life with an expectant attitude looking for real diamonds and not cubic zirconia.

Scripture:

For you created my inmost being; you knit me together in my mother's womb. I praise you because I am fearfully and wonderfully made; your works are wonderful, I know that full well. My frame was not hidden from you when I was made in the secret place, when I was woven together in the depths of the earth. Your eyes saw my unformed body; all the days ordained for me were written in your book before one of them came to be.
Psalm 139: 13-16

Prayer:

Dear Lord in Heaven, please allow me to see myself every single day as you see me. Whether I am meeting potential clients, talking to a bank loan officer, or working in the early morning hours to improve my business, please give me the confidence to face each day knowing that you believe I am valuable. You know I am fearfully and wonderfully made. Would you please help me block the noise from this world and my subconscious voice that tells me anything different?

Call to action:

Write these words on a piece of paper and display it in a place where you will see it daily; *I believe God's word; I am fearfully and wonderfully made.* When you see the note, take a full minute to hold onto those words and govern your actions for the rest of the day guided by this truth.

DAY 2 - WE READY

If you are an aspiring entrepreneur, what is holding you back? We know very well the real and imaginary roadblocks that prevent people from moving forward and becoming legitimate entrepreneurs.

There are usually three reasons for delaying the launch. The first reason is that you really are trying to get things right. You are a perfectionist. If you are building an aircraft or developing a life-saving treatment, being a perfectionist makes sense. Please understand, we are not saying go to market with inferior products. You should also never let bad be a substitute for good. But if it is not a product or service that will cause bodily harm, then we believe perfect is indeed the enemy of the pretty darn good.

The second reason is timing. If you delay and keep waiting until it is just the right time, the right time will never come. There will always be competing interests vying for your attention and battling for your resources. You make time for the things that are important. If launching your business is important, you will carve out the time.

The final reason some of us delay is because we are simply afraid. In reality, we are fearful of criticism and failure. So rather than launch, we fall back on excuses number one and number two. We say it's not perfect or the time is not right.

The truth is that people may criticize you, and you may even fail. But you will never know if you continue to circle in a pattern of fear.

The fact that you are reading this book is proof that we started listening to our own advice. We began working on this book almost a decade ago. Then, in the late fall of 2020, we decided to cast our fears aside and publish it. In the end, we published *Prayer & Pound Cake* because of our firm belief that when business owners begin praying deliberately for their businesses and how God can use them in the marketplace, remarkable changes for good will happen in the world. So, we stopped talking and published because we wanted to be part of that change - WE READY. Are you?

Scripture:
All hard work brings a profit, but mere talk leads only to poverty.
Proverbs 14:23

Prayer:
Dear Lord, I thank you for giving me what I need. You have prepared me for this moment. You are not a God of confusion but a God of order. Order my steps in the path I should go in all areas of my life. Help me to be ready for this chapter of my life. I am seeking you today.

Lord help to avoid excuses as reasons for delaying my dream of starting a business. Please keep my eyes focused on you, and my heart opened to hear you in all decisions I make. Thank you, Lord.

Call to action:
If you have not launched your business or that new product or service, share your idea with a trusted family member or friend. Give them permission to check in with you in one month on your progress.

DAY 3 - FIERCE AND FEARLESS

Few professional endeavors require more courage than starting your own business. Being the boss is not for everyone. But those of us who choose this path, we are inspired, and often terrified by the crazy independence that it brings.

We hold entrepreneurs in such high esteem that sometimes we have to check our enthusiasm. When talking to friends and family about the spirit of an entrepreneur, we should be cautious about making sure we are making a distinction of difference, not a distinction of value. People who go the entrepreneurial route take a different path than their counterparts. It is not a superior path.

In truth, some people work better when they are members of an established team, and it is *not* their name on the door. The world and the marketplace need all types. We sincerely believe it is important to celebrate all kinds of workers. That being said, this book is to celebrate the courage it takes to be an entrepreneur.

To be an entrepreneur, you have to be both fierce and fearless. Whether it is your side hustle or whether you are flying without a net, and it is your full-time job, you by now know that entrepreneurship takes chutzpah.

The key ingredient of being fierce is a savage, unshakable intensity. You will be successful because you are focused and intentional. Successful entrepreneurs are not wishy-washy and lackadaisical about their enterprise. Even when pursuing your business as a side hustle, you have to have a savage, unshakable intensity to accomplish your goals.

The critical component of being fearless is remembering God gave you a spirit of power, which drives out fear every time. Think about it. People with the God-given power are in control and have no reason to fear.

As you grow your business, we hope you have a crowd of people supporting you and cheering you on to success. We will talk about building your tribe. If you don't have a tribe, join our virtual tribe at PrayerAndPoundCake.com and let us cheer for you.

One of our dear friends, Megan Assman-Kool, runs a successful virtual fitness company. She believes you should be your loudest cheerleader. *Mega-Strong Fitness* went from about 20 students online to thousands of students in a matter of months. When clients are working to achieve their fitness goals, Megan often tells them, "Cheer for your own damn self." Don't ever doubt yourself. If there are moments when you have doubt creeping in, remember, not many people are fierce and fearless enough to take an idea and turn it into an entrepreneurial endeavor. You did. So, stop doubting and "Cheer for your own damn self!"

Being fierce and fearless means that you plant your feet, encourage yourself, and move forward. Sometimes the older we get, the more we lose courage because we have had a lifetime of people whispering in our ear, planting doubts and fears. We encourage you to remember the boldness that you had when you were a little girl. Channel that inner child who had no idea that failure was even an option. Bring that fierceness and fearlessness to the table every day when you work on your business.

Scripture:
For the Spirit God gave us does not make us timid, but gives us power, love and self-discipline.
2 Timothy 1:7

"Be strong and very courageous. Be careful to obey all the law my servant Moses gave you; do not turn from it to the right or to the left, that you may be successful wherever you go. Keep this Book of the Law always on your lips; meditate on it day and night, so that you may be careful to do everything written in it. Then you will be prosperous and successful. Have I not commanded you? Be strong and courageous. Do not be afraid; do not be discouraged, for the Lord your God will be with you wherever you go."
Joshua 1: 7-9

Prayer:
Lord, anytime I am afraid or uncertainty enters my mind, I pray that I am quickly reminded of your words. Thank you for your gift of power, love and a sound mind. What amazing gifts. I want to use the gifts of power, love, and a sound mind to be fierce and fearless as I build my business. I have the power to tackle any obstacle placed before me. I will make fierce, fearless, and wise decisions because of the sound mind you have given me. God, I have every single thing I need to grow this business and glorify you. I will NOT be afraid. I WILL put all my trust in you, Lord.

Call to action:
Make a list of every time you have been anxious or fearful about a business issue and record how the Lord allowed you to survive and even thrive beyond that challenge. Take heart and have courage because the challenges before you today will also be conquered by the Lord. Do not fear. He was faithful then. He is faithful today. He will be faithful tomorrow.

DAY 4 - KNOW YOUR VALUE

Without question, not placing high value or even market value on our services is the biggest mistake we have made in business. In the early days, we spent too much money on an elaborate phone system. We spent more on parking than rent by first opening an office in Georgetown, one of the most expensive neighborhoods in Washington, D.C. We took forever to invest in top-line business cards. We neglected to always follow up with handwritten thank you notes.

The list of early foibles is long. But the error from which we have taken the longest to recover is placing too low a value on who we are and what we do. Our poster child one-percenters are not ashamed, afraid, intimidated by, or confused about who they are or the value of their gift.

The excuse we gave ourselves for undercutting or lowering our rates was that it was loss leader pricing. We rationalized the strategic pricing of selling our services at a loss to attract more customers. Business owners certainly should employ strategic pricing. Using loss leaders to attract more business is a long-tested method.

But please, trust us our experience. Once you set your rates low, they stay there. Do not make the mistake of pricing your main products and services as if they are loss leaders. If you fear losing a client because they are unwilling to pay you the fair market value for your goods and services, they are better off using your competitor.

Customers who fight you on your rates do not value your expertise. In our experience, they are the gems who call you an hour past closing on a Friday with tasks that are urgent only in their minds. We promise, you and your business are better off without them. Life is better without them.

Determining your rates is not guesswork. Precise pricing science exists to help you understand the rates that your field and market can bear.

We offer a special word to fellow consultants: Consultant is not a dirty word. Yes, we parachute in and out, often making full-time staff a tad squeamish. But with the consultant title, many clients think they can haggle on our prices as if they are bartering at an open-air flea market.

Clients will try to reduce your rates because you make it look so easy. It looks so easy because you know exactly what you are doing.

One of our favorite consultant stories is told with a couple of variations. In one version, it is a malfunctioning submarine. In the version we like best, it is a malfunctioning printing press.

Before a prominent New York City newspaper was preparing to print advertisements and coupons for Black Friday, its printing press began to have fits. This is, of course, a nightmare because Black Friday is one of the most profitable days of the retail and advertising year.

The young technicians in the print shop tried everything they could to fix the printing press, but the nearly 60 year old equipment would not cooperate. It appeared to be busted with no avenue for repair. Finally, the situation became so dire that the owner of the paper was alerted. He remembered Jerry, a former employee who had long since retired.

The owner said, "Get Jerry on the line. If he can't fix it, no one can."

So, the production manager called Jerry, making apologies for the hour. The urgency in his voice made it clear to Jerry that they had tried everything and were at their wits' end. Jerry, having spent a wonderful Thanksgiving with his family, told the manager not to worry. He would be right over.

When Jerry arrived, the room was filled with young, clueless technicians. The old expert walked around the giant machine, stood back, walked to the dashboard of buttons and widgets. He pressed one button, and the printing press began to roar. The room erupted in cheers and laughter. They were back in business and were able to print the newspaper for the next edition.

The following week the owner received a letter in the mail from Jerry thanking him for the business. He also enclosed his invoice for $10,000. The owner was outraged. Jerry had been there for two minutes, maybe five minutes max. The owner called Jerry and asked him to send an itemized invoice. He believed that when forced to itemize his services, Jerry would reduce his rates.

Jerry quickly replied with the new invoice. There were two line items listed, $1 for pushing the button and $9,999 for knowing which button to push.

You know which button to push in your business. Set your rates accordingly, and do not back down. You know your value.

Scripture:
But blessed is the one who trusts in the Lord, whose confidence is in him.
Jeremiah 17:7

But God demonstrates His own love for us in this: While we were still sinners, Christ died for us.
Romans 5:8

Prayer:

I come to you today, Lord, to say thank you again. Thank you for loving me. I believe I am valuable because your word says so. I believe in my abilities because my gifts come from you, Lord. You believe that I am valuable and demonstrated it by sending Christ to bear the weight of my wrongs. When I sell myself short, I am selling you short. Please, God, do not ever allow me to diminish my worth. Let me trust in what you believe about me.

Call to action:

Take time to review your rates and prices to ensure you are not undervaluing yourself and your products.

DAY 5 - OWN THE EXCELLENCE

For the past decade, our exercise of choice has been running. Dee Dee and her husband, Brian, are winter runners braving races when the weather is near or below freezing. Deana and her husband La Forrest enjoy spring weather runs. Deana ran her first marathon when she was 30 years old and her second marathon nine years later. In between, there were 10 milers, half marathons and countless 5ks and 10ks. After marathon number two, she bought bumper stickers with the distance 26.2 to mark the milestone.

But even after buying the brag tags, she still refused to call herself a runner. Instead, her response to any question about running would be, "Oh, I run, but I'm not a *runner*." Or "Oh, I'm no speed demon. I'm not a *real* runner."

One Friday night, as a group of volunteers from her church loaded into her car to head out to feed the homeless in downtown Washington, D.C., one of the volunteers saw the tags and said, "Wow, you've run a marathon? That's so cool. I would love to be a runner."

Of course, Deana replied with a version of the old refrain, "Running is my exercise of choice. But I'm not a real runner."

The girl, a stranger to Deana, looked at her in complete bewilderment. "So, how many marathons have you run?"

"Only two," Deana replied.

"How often do you run?" the girl asked.

"Oh, I run at least five times a week," Deana said.

The girl smiled and said, "Well, I think that makes you a runner."

She was right. Deana is a runner. She is not as fast as she wants to be but running five days a week has made her faster than she ever was.

In business, this propensity to downplay your talents is deadly. If Deana were to respond to people about her role as a public relations professional the way she responded about her running accomplishments, who on earth would want to hire her? "Oh, I spend five days a week working in PR, but I'm not *really* a publicist."

We want to be clear on the difference between owning your excellence and being a braggart. When Dee Dee turned 40, to celebrate, she ran in a 5k race. She placed first in her age group. What an accomplishment! She celebrated by giving glory to God. She gave glory to God that she could soar on wings like eagles and in doing so, she inspired others to start running. She did not boast about her ability. Instead, she celebrated the work that God had done in her.

No one likes a glory goat. The insecure or overconfident boastings of a glory goat are very different from the joyous praise of someone honoring God for their gifts and blessings. The former repels people. The latter attracts people. Be the person who gives honor to God and attracts.

Scripture:

In the same way, let your light shine before others, that they may see your good deeds and glorify your Father in heaven. Matthew 5:16

Prayer:

Dear Lord, help me speak positively when referring to the gifts you have given me. I do not want to merely project a positive image; I want to be the positive force wherever I am. Let me not celebrate my gifts to bring glory to my own life and business. Instead, let me bring glory to you. May you receive every ounce of glory and honor for any success.

Call to action:

Take time today and make a list of areas where you mock or diminish your accomplishments. Consider why you are reluctant to celebrate yourself in these areas? Think of ways to celebrate your talent while sincerely praising God for this gift. Avoid humble bragging. Share your success boldly. Commit to letting your light shine in those areas so that your Father in Heaven will receive glory.

DAY 6 - MENTOR VS. SPONSOR

Do you know the difference between a mentor and a sponsor? Both are extremely valuable. However, the roles they play are quite different. A mentor is someone who shares knowledge with you and offers constructive criticism on your career goals and performance. Sometimes, a mentor has earned the right to offer wise counsel simply because they have had your back and have seen you through the rough spots in life and business.

On the other hand, a sponsor is someone who does those things, in addition, to providing opportunities and opening doors. In our life, we have had the blessing of countless mentors but very few sponsors. One is not necessarily more valuable than the other. However, it is crucial to understand the difference.

A sponsor is someone who will put their name on the line to co-sign your future success. If you are unclear on the difference, you may become bitter because you expect mentors to behave like sponsors when that is not their role or goal. We should soak up all of the knowledge, insight and wisdom that we can from our mentors. Having access to sit at the foot of the wise should not be taken for granted. Soaking up and implementing the insight gained from a mentor's hard-earned lived experiences will bring your business success.

Additionally, we should capitalize on every opened door, new contact and tangible resource our sponsors provide. Being given access to the inner circle and advantage to job opportunities because someone vouches for you is not to be taken lightly. In reality, this is the advantage that those born into the one-percent have over the rest of the world.

What some falsely identify as overt racism is nothing more than benign access. This is a lesson to sponsors. If you are opening doors to the c-suite for those in your network and your network is homogeneous, the diversity of the c-suite will not change.

Choose your mentors and sponsors wisely. Do not take advice from everyone willing to give it. If you want to operate a business of integrity, do not seek counsel from business leaders who cut corners or treat their employees with scorn. Business leaders who have achieved success are ideal as mentors, but business leaders who have recovered from failures are even more important. Learn from the missteps of your wise counselors.

You may naturally gain a mentor through family friendships, work, school or a network like your sorority or fraternity. If your network doesn't naturally yield a mentor, identify a successful business leader and reach out to them. They may think you are nuts and say no. But they may admire your chutzpah and be flattered. Another resource is SCORE.org. They have a database of volunteers from all business sectors who are waiting to mentor you.

Scripture:

For lack of guidance a nation falls, but victory is won through many advisers.
Proverbs 11:14

So we cared for you. Because we loved you so much, we were delighted to share with you not only the gospel of God but our lives as well.
1 Thessalonians 2:8

This is what the Lord Almighty says: "Do not listen to what the prophets are prophesying to you; they fill you with false hopes. They speak visions from their own minds, not from the mouth of the Lord."
Jeremiah 23:16

Walk with the wise and become wise, for a companion of fools suffers harm.
Proverbs 13:20

Prayer:
Heavenly Father, I pray for mentors to offer wise counsel and sponsors to help open doors. I pray for amazing blessings to impact their businesses because of their generosity to me. As I pray for mentors and sponsors, I ask that you help me to be the same right now for business owners who would benefit from my knowledge and business understanding. I pray for an ever-growing circle of Christian business owners impacting the marketplace with services and attitudes that bring you honor.

Call to action:
Take time today to call, text or email people who have served as mentors and sponsors in your life. Show gratitude with the sole purpose of showing gratitude. When you have thanked your mentors and sponsors, identify someone whom you may pour into as a mentor or sponsor.

DAY 7 - READ FOR YOUR LIFE

We grew up in a house filled with books. Even today, when we go to our mama's house, books spill from every table in every room: literary classics, business books, cookbooks, books on American history, and international travel. We often take for granted what it meant to our personal and professional maturation to grow up in a working-class house brimming with books. Books are expensive. But it is a worthy expense because those who read consume knowledge, and it is life-altering.

As a result of our childhood exposure to books, we have continued to read throughout our adulthood. Dee Dee loves the feel of an actual physical book in her hands. Deana is addicted to audiobooks. We believe there are too many platforms and delivery methods to find excuses for not reading for your life. With all of the delivery methods, one will suit you and the way you best consume data.

We have included this section because, as business owners, reading for your life is critical in two areas. First, it is an excellent source of professional development. Second, it is a beautiful method of relaxation. We are better businesswomen because of consuming the works of business pros like Mike Michalowicz and William F. Pickard. But for every non-fiction business book we read, we also grow and rest in the fictional works of Dwayne Alexander Smith, B.A. Paris and other delicious literary escape artists.

While we read both books for business and books for pleasure, reading for your life means reading, at this point, whatever you can. Reading expands your vocabulary and expands your knowledge of the world around you and the world beyond you.

We believe reading the Bible is a great benefit to Christian business owners and non-Christian business owners. For Christian business owners, it should serve as your professional and personal guidebook. For non-Christian business owners, the lessons on morality and world history will only make you wiser.

At PrayerAndPoundCake.com, we link to areas where you may read and listen to the Bible and other books. Our favorite is LibriVox, which is a source for free audiobooks that are in the public domain. You can read from a wide variety of works. You can also download free electronic books to your smartphone or your iPad through the Kindle.

The wealthy have libraries. The poor have flat-screen televisions. Over the years, as we have entered the homes of friends and colleagues who are successful in business, the common denominator is that their homes are brimming with books.

Scripture:
Until I come, devote yourself to the public reading of Scripture, to preaching and to teaching.
1Timothy 4:13

Your word is a lamp for my feet, and a light on my path.
Psalm 119:105

Prayer:
I want to be knowledgeable in all things that pertain to my business. I need your help, Lord. Please show me what lessons I need to consume to grow my business. Are there

classes I need to take and books I need to read? Whatever it takes, Lord, I am ready and willing. Please show me the way. Please help me to be diligent and not give up.

Heavenly Father, please let me be even more diligent in reading your word and understanding the lessons found in Scripture. As I pursue knowledge to feed my professional development, Father, let me clearly understand that my most important business is seeking you. I know your word will clear away confusion and deliver enlightening knowledge in all parts of my life.

Call to action:
Visit PrayerAndPoundCake.com and download our resource for free books.

MIND YOUR BUSINESS

*Concentrate all your thoughts upon the work at hand. The sun's rays
do not burn until brought to a focus.*

ALEXANDER GRAHAM BELL

DAY 8 - PASSION, PERFORMANCE AND PROFIT

Our daily work is public relations and public affairs. Visit us at PolicyAndPoundCake.com and BassPublicAffairs.com to learn more about the work that we do in these fields. While our daily vocation is not in the ministry, our devotion to Christ makes every project we accept an opportunity to bring honor to Christ. We don't always succeed, but it is our ultimate motive.

As people who follow Christ, we believe committing to work that honors him should be our priority. After that essential bar is met, we believe there are three areas you must consider when determining the business you will pursue. They are passion, performance and profit. The most successful businesses excel in all three.

- Passion - You must have the desire to accomplish your mission.
- Performance - You must have the ability to accomplish your mission.
- Profit - You must have the capacity to make a profit by accomplishing your mission.

Passion:

Confucius once said, "Choose a job you love, and you'll never work a day in your life." As wonderful as that sounds, it isn't true. Work is always work, even when you love it. But we do believe when you love what you do, the

38

drudgery, the little laborious nature of work is not as burdensome.

If you love to bake cakes, and you would bake cakes even if people did not pay you to do it, you may have found your passion.

The most successful entrepreneurs are pursuing their passion. In his book, *The Virgin Way: Everything I Know About Leadership,* passionate Virgin Group founder Richard Branson wrote, "The first thing that has to be recognized is that one cannot train someone to be passionate--it's either in their DNA, or it's not."

At Bass Public Affairs, we are passionate about altruistic missions. If you want to house the homeless, advance opportunities for the underprivileged or empower small business owners, we are the firm for you. If your mission is to sell fancy and impressive widgets, we will likely take a pass at the work. If you are entering into a business venture that does not excite you, we encourage you to step back and examine where your passion lives.

Performance:

Unfortunately, sometimes as we define our passion, there is a bittersweet pill to swallow because we may have to realize that our performance does not match our passion. For example, you may have a passion for painting landscapes, but your performance for painting landscapes is less than stellar. In this situation, you have a few options. You can move on to identify another passion or invest in yourself to get the training necessary to perform with excellence.

Malcolm Gladwell wrote in his 2008 book, *Outliers,* "ten thousand hours is the magic number of greatness." By this estimate, it would take you 1,250 days working eight hours each day to reach greatness at landscape painting. Do you have the time and the patience to put in the hours for the performance?

We like Gladwell's ballpark, but we recognize it is not a perfect number. It does not consider natural talents and natural ineptitude. Raw talent may get you to an expert level in fewer than 10,000 hours. But the harsh reality is that if we have no skill in our passion, no number of hours may equip us to excel at what we love to do most.

Profit:

The third and equally important piece to the mission equation is profit. Most of us will agree without reservation that we are in business to make money. We may have a noble passion and the ability to perform, but the bottom line is, if we are not making money, we are not a successful business. We may be a successful non-profit, but not a successful business. Also, no one goes into business to go into debt.

In the beginning, your business may struggle to make a profit. You are growing your brand, building your audience, experimenting with products and services. But if you are always in a cat and dog fight struggling to squeeze out a penny every single year, you have to be serious about knowing when to "fold 'em." There could be many reasons why you are not pulling in a profit. Therefore, it is essential to determine the realistic revenue potential that your business offers.

Dee Dee is the profit-and-loss manager of our business. In 2015, we launched GROWTHComms, a communications conference for faith-based organizations. Because we encountered countless churches that did not generate high-quality communications, GROWTHComms offered church leaders direct access to media relations training.

We had the passion for helping people share what we believe is the most important message the world has ever known. Working with the nation's top communications professionals, we wanted to help Christian organizations step up their communications game. However, Dee Dee recognized that GROWTHComms did not generate enough profit to make it something we could continue doing. She decided to stop hosting GROWTHComms because, while we have a charitable mission, we are not a charity.

When you are doing work that you believe is noble, it may seem greedy and selfish to end work that is not profitable. In reality, if you find that one area of your work is not profitable, you may be risking the success of other divisions of your business. It costs you time and resources better spent elsewhere. As wonderful as GROWTHComms was, Dee Dee recognized that it took too much time away from other profitable areas.

The three Ps are as simple as they are profound. If you do not have passion, cannot show performance, and do not generate a profit, your road to success is a rollercoaster of chaos—and may go off the rails.

Scripture:
Do not be anxious about anything, but in every situation, by prayer and petition, with thanksgiving, present your requests to God.
Philippians 4:6

Whatever you do, work at it with all your heart, as working for the Lord, not for human masters, 24 since you know that you will receive an inheritance from the Lord as a reward. It is the Lord Christ you are serving.
Colossians 3:23

Prayer:
Dear Lord, I ask for wisdom as I examine my passion, performance, and ability to generate profit. Please help me to be realistic about my performance in these areas. Lord, I am seeking your guidance, and I thank you in advance for your wisdom and grace.

Call to action:
Whether you have launched your business or are preparing to launch it, it is important to seriously evaluate your passion, performance, and profit. Do not be anxious but pray and give thanks.

DAY 9 - CHARTING YOUR COURSE

Most people go into business because they have a bright idea. However, they do not have a vision or a mission. A vision is an aspirational state of a future world you want to create. A mission is your company's reason for being.

When we started Bass Public Affairs, we did not have a vision or a mission. We had quite a few bright ideas. We both kept what we called our *Bright Idea Journals.* Dee Dee had a journal in Delaware, and Deana kept a matching journal in Washington, D.C.

In these journals, we wrote down every possible idea for a business. No idea was too far-fetched or outrageous. Once we settled on our business idea, a public relations firm, we determined a mission.

Our early mission was to provide small and mid-sized businesses with earned, owned and paid media tools to reach their target audiences. There is nothing particularly earth-shattering about this mission. However, as basic as the mission was, it gave us marching orders and directions. Now that we have been in business for over 15 years, we have made slight adjustments to our mission. Our portfolio now includes not only small businesses but also fortune 500s and national and global organizations. Our list of services in the three media categories is now even more detailed and granular.

Unfortunately, far too many small business owners skip writing a clear mission statement. Even fewer bother to take the time to write a proper business plan. The company's mission statement is one of the first things you share in your business plan's executive summary.

We are all about cost savings, so we would say, if you are not seeking investors, it is not necessary to pay a professional to draft a formal business plan for you. But we do believe it is important to create a tangible record of who you are and what you want to do. In the coming days, we will emphasize how so much rides on the clarity of your mission. Trust our experience. It is important to go through the exercise of expressing your clearly defined vision and mission.

Scripture:
Then the Lord replied: "Write down the revelation and make it plain on tablets so that a herald may run with it." Habakkuk 2:2

Prayer:
Father, I am praying right now that the vision for my business is crystal clear.

Dear Lord, order my steps. You know the desires of my heart. I want to please you, Lord. If I am going in the wrong direction, please, Lord, make it plain. If this is what you want me to do, make it crystal clear. If the plans I have made are not according to your will, I will change my plans, and I will follow you. I want your vision, Lord, not my own.

Call to action:
Visit PrayerAndPoundCake.com and gain access to online business plan templates. Then, give yourself a reasonable deadline to complete your business plan. You should have it completed by the time you finish this book!

DAY 10 - MARKET ANALYSIS

You would be surprised by the number of people who start a business simply because they think they have a great idea. The fact that there is nothing new under the sun is the best reason to do a market analysis before launching into a new business. Many entrepreneurs have a great idea but do not do the due diligence to see what the market says about their idea.

In his 2015 TED Talk, Idealab founder Bill Gross shared insight on the top five reasons startups succeed or fail. Idealab studied 200 companies and found that 42 percent attributed timing to the success or failure of their business. An idea can be great, and the execution could be masterful, but timing played the most significant factor in their success. A market analysis will let you know if your timing is right.

Gross highlights Airbnb as a great idea. However, before 2008, not many people would have considered temporarily renting out rooms in their homes to strangers. The recession made the timing right for homeowners looking to leverage their property as a revenue source and travelers looking for cost-effective accommodations.

A market analysis is as vital as your business plan. If you have the budget in place, you can hire a firm. If you do not have the budget, there are many tools and resources to help you conduct your market analysis.

We caution you, do not conduct a market analysis to simply check the box. Also, don't twist the data to mean what you want it to mean. This is like those times when we say, "Let me pray about it," knowing fully that we have made up our minds on an action long before we go to prayer.

Before you begin your market analysis, you should resolve to accept the results of the research. For example, suppose your market analysis determines that the market is already oversaturated, and your business idea or concept is not needed and will struggle among stiff competition. In that case, you have to be willing to make the necessary adjustments suggested by the analysis, put a hold on your business until the market has room for it or maybe even walk away from the project altogether. Sometimes walking away is the hardest thing for an entrepreneur to do.

It may happen in the movies, but in real life you should not just hang up your shingle on guts alone. A market analysis will let you know if there are other companies with the same bright idea. Another company with the same service or product may be just down the road or one click away on the Internet.

Of course, just because hundreds of companies already provide the kind of product or service you have in mind does not mean your only alternative is to abandon your dream. On the contrary, it may cause you to improve the idea you had, making it more profitable than you initially imagined.

Your market analysis will tell you a great deal about your competition. But as necessary as it is to learn about the existing competition, it is also essential to learn about the people and organizations that started and failed. A market analysis will tell you who has attempted to do what you are trying to do now. You can learn from their mistakes. If they are no longer in business, they might even be interested in advising you about the areas they found difficult.

Once we settled on the business to pursue, we did our due diligence to conduct a market analysis. The type of market analysis that we perform today is far more sophisticated, with impressive software and bells and whistles. But the nuts and bolts analysis we conducted 15 years ago was more than sufficient to tell us that we were launching something profitable.

The market analysis identified hundreds of public affairs firms of all shapes and sizes. However, not one firm was focused on our specific market niche. The niche gave us the competitive edge needed to be different, stand out and succeed.

Scripture:
What has been will be again, what has been done will be done again; there is nothing new under the sun.
Ecclesiastes 1:9

Prayer:
Lord, please help me to listen to the numbers. Help me to research and investigate to learn more about my industry. Dear Lord, help me to distinguish my business from the pack.

I want to understand all avenues of this journey, Lord. But whatever I do not understand, I pray you give me the wisdom to ask for help from those who do understand. Give me the humility to ask for help from people who have tried and succeeded in my field and from people who have tried and had negative results. Bless them in their hearts to be open to sharing their knowledge with me, Lord. Open my heart to receive wise counsel.

Call to action:
Visit PrayerAndPoundCake.com and download a market analysis framework.

DAY 11 - YOUR LANE IS A SUPERHIGHWAY

If we refuse to establish a laser-focused mission, we allow ourselves and our business to become everything for everybody. The result is burnout and bust.

When you are clear and focused on what your mission is, every other task finds its place of priority and necessity. If your mission is clear, your target audience is evident and the people you must pursue to accomplish your mission are obvious.

When we first started Bass Public Affairs, we wanted to be a media firm that handled everything related to communications for small and mid-sized companies. We tackled all owned, earned, and paid media falling under any legal and moral banner. The categories could be sports, entertainment, political, Christian or African-American media. For large shops this is not uncommon.

We did not have the luxury of tackling every topic with expertise. However, in the early days, turning away a client seemed nothing short of ludicrous. We did not want to turn away anyone who wanted to hire us to pursue media or develop a communications strategy. In those early days, we were in the business of surviving. We soon learned, however, that decisions you make to survive do not necessarily make you grow.

Sometimes saying no, takes more courage than saying yes. We were acting out of a spirit of fear. Our fear was if we did not take the client, we would miss out on revenue when revenue was scarce. Lack of clarity in your business vision often comes from standing in a place of fear. Is it possible that fear is keeping you from establishing a laser-focused mission?

Bass Public Affairs spent four good years not being laser-focused. In not being laser-focused, we took on wonderful clients, who were disastrous fits. One of our most impressive clients was a cyber security firm. The goal was to garner earned media for the CEO of the firm. We began to pursue cyber security media outlets and cyber security reporters but quickly discovered we were out of our lane. Neither of us had a background or interest in cyber security. We spent precious time trying to understand basic concepts to have conversations with journalists who were knee-deep in the issue every day.

One option would be to outsource. If we had been able to staff ourselves with a cyber security expert communicator, our performance would have improved. However, it would have done nothing to ignite our passion. Not only did we not have the capacity to speak the cyber security language, but we also did not even have the heart for it. The result was a failure for us and the client. The daily stress of knowing that you do not know what you are doing is the icing on a poop cake.

As disappointed as we were to lose the monthly retainer, there was an enormous burden lifted because, at last, we were not stuck doing what we did not have the ability or desire to do. Looking back, we believe we lost business by spinning our wheels on cyber security issues. We wasted time figuring out how to do work for the wrong client that would have been better spent pursuing the right clients.

When you have a clear mission, you will know your lane. When you think of your lane, do not think of a tiny backroad. Instead, imagine the wide lane on a massive highway—one with plenty of room for many clients.

Because of our painful experience in cyber security, Bass Public Affairs is now exclusively focused on clients whose work falls under what we call an opportunity agenda. Our sweet spot is communications for clients who ultimately have altruistic goals to empower underrepresented communities. This superhighway lane is broad enough to accommodate clients ranging from national non-profits that create jobs for homeless veterans to international corporations developing mixed-use housing for low to moderate-income families.

We know our lane. It is a superhighway of diverse clients. Knowing our lane sets our priorities and makes our direction clear.

Scripture:
And God is able to bless you abundantly, so that in all things at all times, having all that you need, you will abound in every good work.
2 Corinthians 9:8

Therefore, I tell you, do not worry about your life, what you will eat or drink; or about your body, what you will wear. Is not life more than food, and the body more than clothes? Look at the birds of the air; they do not sow or reap or store away in barns, and yet your heavenly Father feeds them. Are you not much more valuable than they? Can any one of you, by worrying, add a single hour to your life?
Matthew 6:25-27

Prayer:
Father, please give me the courage to stay in my lane. Please give me the faith to see that my lane is a superhighway of possibilities. Do not allow me to operate in fear by taking on clients or business ventures outside my lane. I want to tackle the work that is best suited for me to succeed. Father, keep

me focused on what I do well and not on endeavors that will take me away from my mission and gifts.

Call to action:

Take a hard look at your clients, products and services. Determine which areas are in your lane and which areas are not in your lane. If you find that you are outside of your scope and ability, pray for wisdom on how to grow your business to replace that income with income-driven from areas within your area of expertise.

DAY 12 - MAY I GET THAT IN WRITING?

Many small business owners work on the strength of their good name and trusted word. Our word is our bond. A handshake means it is a deal. But we understand in legal realms, an agreement is only as strong as the terms in a contract.

In reality, if you do not have a contract to guarantee and define your services, you are at a disadvantage when confusion or disagreements arise. Contracts are important for spelling out the scope of work with people you have done business with in the past as well as with new clients.

We have had very few occasions where someone has tried to break the original agreed upon scope of services, but we believe the reason we have not fallen into that trap is because we do use contracts.

We have a standard contract for our basic services that we call our tools of engagement. So, when we enter into a new relationship, we pull out the tools of engagement template, and we adjust the document for the new agreement. Sometimes, we add items to it, sometimes we take items away. However, because we have our standard tools of engagement, we pretty much know how best to pitch our services and our prices.

Furthermore, we are very comfortable with the language of our tools of engagement. However, there are cases when we are working with a much larger organization that require that we sign their contract. In some cases, these contracts can be long and tedious. Whether it is your template contract or the contract of a corporate client, you must read and understand what you are signing.

Never be shy or embarrassed to ask questions about areas of a contract that you do not understand. It is important to discuss these areas with your potential client, and in some cases, you may have to discuss these areas with an attorney. The worst thing to do is sign a contract that you have not read and do not understand.

Contracts are important because they protect you and the integrity of your work. They protect your employees. We can give you some nightmare examples of people who lost it all because they did not have a contract.

When you are doing business with family or friends, sometimes you may feel awkward about actually asking them to sign a contract. First of all, if someone is offended by being asked to sign a contract, you should consider that a red flag. The contract protects them as much as it protects you.

Clarity is essential in business relationships. A contract clarifies the work, the product, the deliverables and the goals.

Scripture:
All you need to say is simply 'Yes' or 'No'; anything beyond this comes from the evil one.
Matthew 5:37

Prayer:
Dear Lord, I want to go into each client relationship with all parties knowing and understanding the expectations. My prayer, Lord, is that you remove all the awkward feelings that may come when it is time to discuss finances and deliverables. I pray that those at the negotiating table offer and receive fair treatment and respect. I pray that each

business transaction brings honor to you because of the integrity of all parties involved.

Call to action:
Visit PrayerAndPoundCake.com for contract resources.

DAY 13 - GETTING PAID

For Dee Dee, the approach to pricing Bass Public Affairs services has always been straightforward. Her first job out of college was working in corporate America in revenue recoupment. Yes, she was one of those highly unpleasant people who called to remind you to pay your credit card bill. In her early twenties, Dee Dee spent 40 plus hours a week telling the very rich and the very poor to pay for their outstanding bills. Maybe she did not rack up Malcolm Gladwell's 10,000 hours to qualify her as an expert. But she certainly logged enough hours to make her comfortable planting her feet and saying in no uncertain terms, "You owe us money. Pay now." Her name around Bass Public Affairs circles is the collection artist. Trust us. Collections is an art form.

The second reason Dee Dee is good at asking clients for money is directly related to the little mouths that she must feed. Dee Dee's priority is providing for two real-life human beings. Asking clients to pay or else gets easy when she is thinking about her children. Deana's ability to survive on peanut butter and jelly contributes to her reluctance to recoup delinquent funds aggressively.

It does not matter why you have the good sense, chutzpah or guts to get delinquent clients to pay. The bottom line is that you make sure someone in the company is equipped to do it.

There are systems that you can put in place to automate payments. Rather than list them here only for them to be outdated at the time of printing, visit our website PrayerAndPoundCake.com.

Getting paid is one of the most overlooked aspects of starting a business. As entrepreneurs, we put effort into planning our launch strategy, developing our products, fine-tuning our sales pitch, but sometimes we overlook the actual procedure and protocol of getting paid. In today's age of mobile apps and smartphones, there are many easy and cost-effective ways for you to get your money.

Research to determine what are the standard payment methods for your industry. Take care to avoid any method of payment that will charge you an excessive merchant fee.

Also, make sure you understand the best-practice length of time to be paid. For example, does your industry operate on a net thirty, net sixty or, heaven forbid, a net ninety rule?

Investigate the best ways to alert your clients that their bill is coming due. Sending helpful reminders is one way. Make sure that these terms are spelled out clearly in your contract. In addition, you should consider offering perks for paying in advance or paying all at once.

We do not encourage you to use a heavy, disrespectful hand when dealing with late clients, but we encourage you to be firm.

Many small businesses go into debt and have to close their doors because they have allowed clients to go months and, in some cases, even years without paying. You are not running a charity, and it is perfectly in your right to insist that you be paid.

Remember, the street goes both ways. Make it a practice to pay your employees, vendors and consultants on time. The most fun that Dee Dee has in a month is when she signs the front of the checks and pays Bass Public Affairs' consultants. Creating revenue for yourself and your family is an unbelievable blessing; creating jobs and revenue for others is an entrepreneur's dream.

Scripture:
Give to everyone what you owe them: If you owe taxes, pay taxes; if revenue, then revenue; if respect, then respect; if honor, then honor. Let no debt remain outstanding, except the continuing debt to love one another, for whoever loves others has fulfilled the law.
Romans 13:7-8

Do not withhold good from those to whom it is due, when it is in your power to do it. Do not say to your neighbor, "come back tomorrow I'll give it to you"- when you already have it with you.
Proverbs 3:27-28

Prayer:
Dear Lord, I pray every conversation I have about being paid by clients and paying employees is filled with mutual respect, honesty and clarity. I will walk away from each conversation with peace because I will walk into each conversation full of integrity and fairness.

Father, I offer gratitude and praise for clients who pay early and on time. Thank you for the financial blessing that their diligence means to me and my family.

Please give me the wisdom not to enter into business relationships with employees I do not have the financial ability to pay. When it is time for me to pay those who I owe, please let me be known for paying early and on time.

Call to action:
Review your outstanding balances. If you owe vendors or employees, make arrangements to pay them. If some customers or clients owe you, approach them with confidence and compassion. Before you make the call, be sure that you are clear on the circumstances, the contract agreement, the products, and services provided.

DAY 14 - MISSION CREEP

We know you will be heeding our warning and will be using clean and clear contracts for all of the services you offer. However, it is often important to examine contracts to assess whether you are experiencing the often-hidden problem, mission creep.

Mission creep occurs little by little, day by day, until after months of work, the services you are delivering in no way resemble services defined in the contract's statement of work. The term first arose when describing a common phenomenon afflicting military operations. When an initial campaign found success or appeared to need adjustments to achieve success, additional assignments were piled on until the troops found themselves bogged down with responsibilities far removed from their original mission.

The consequences of mission creep are probably far less dramatic in your business than they are in military operations. But for success, it is crucial to tackle mission creep, nonetheless. Usually, the consultant or service provider is on the losing end of mission creep. You begin doing extra work not addressed in the contract for the good of the project. You may have intended it to be a one-time expansion of services. In mission creep, rather than stopping to revise the contract to include that service, you perform that service. Over time, you continue to perform that service to the point where the client mentally begins to think that they are paying for that service. They are, of course, *not* paying for it. You're giving it to them for free.

In such cases, when you believe performing an additional service will be good for the project, do not let it go undocumented. In your monthly invoice, include the additional services that you have offered; note what you would typically charge for those services, but mark them as "complementary" on the invoice. This is an opportunity for you to ask the client if they would like to continue the services. If they would like to continue that service, revise the scope of work to reflect the change.

The actual danger of mission creep is moving so far away from the initially intended plan that you don't accomplish the work specified in the contract. If you are not delivering what is in the contract at the end of the day, the shortfall will be your problem.

Mission creep happens to consultants who provide a service, but it can just as easily happen to a business owner who offers a product. For example, if your mission to your customers is to provide the best soul food in the city, but there is an opportunity to include Korean food or fast food or vegan food on your menu, it may be a brilliant idea. But it is also very likely mission creep.

You may get away with mission creep for a short time, but eventually, mission creep will result in a mission not accomplished.

We have experienced mission creep in our work endeavors. However, one of the clearest examples that we can share with you is in our life as Christians. In Matthew 28:19, Paul shares the great commission. Our mission is crystal clear, "Go make disciples." Our good intentions have us doing a dozen other things. Some of the work is noble, but it is all a distraction if we are not making disciples.

The same is true for your work endeavors. If you are adding services but not completing the intended mission, you are not fulfilling the contract. If you are adding new products but not fulfilling your commitment to customers, you may have a version of mission creep. Understand the dilemma of mission creep, both for you and your client. We believe the best way to avoid mission creep is to review the contract often and stick to the services in the contract.

Scripture:

Then the eleven disciples went to Galilee, to the mountain where Jesus had told them to go. When they saw him, they worshiped him; but some doubted. Then Jesus came to them and said, "All authority in Heaven and on earth has been given to me. Therefore go and make disciples of all nations, baptizing them in the name of the Father and of the Son and of the Holy Spirit, and teaching them to obey everything I have commanded you. And surely, I am with you always, to the very end of the age."
Matthew 28:16-20

Prayer:

Father, please help me to stay focused on the mission you have given me for my business. If I am tempted to veer to the left or the right, I ask for discipline and patience to keep moving forward in the direction that you have given me.

I also pray for the discipline to stay focused on the specific objectives I agreed to accomplish for my customers and clients. I want to honor my word and contract to deliver what I promised. As new opportunities arise, let me evaluate them with wisdom and focus on accomplishing the actual mission.

Call to action:

Review your contracts with clients and your commitment to customers. Look at the scope of work and the intended goal. If your day-to-day work has moved away from that mission, make clear plans to course correct.

DAY 15 - WORKING FROM HOME

COVID-19 gave companies around the globe the freedom to ditch the office and work from home. In January 2020, Gallup.com shared a study reporting 54 percent of employees said they would "change jobs for the choice to work remotely or not." By March 2020, courtesy of COVID-19, many were getting the chance to work remotely. COVID-19 proved that many businesses could survive and even thrive by having a large number of employees teleworking. Businesses found that their employees were as productive, if not even more productive, working at home. In addition to improvements in productivity, there have been benefits to the environment as well.

Working from home is nothing new for entrepreneurs. According to data from the Small Business Administration, 52 percent of small businesses primarily operate out of the home. For many consultants like Bass Public Affairs, it is easy to do work wherever there's the Internet. While we maintain an office in Washington, D.C., we are just as productive working from our homes.

There are a couple of things that can help to make your work environment productive. First, make sure you have a dedicated space for your work. Whether your home is large or small, it is all too easy to have your work spill from room to room. You can help maintain order—and sanity—

in your life if you allow one area to be your dedicated workspace.

We also recommend that you have dedicated work time. The regular time may be nine to five. If you're not full-time with your business, it may be three hours every Tuesday or whatever consistent time suits you. Whatever it is, keep your business tamed so that it doesn't spill over into your personal and family time. If you work from home, it's easy to allow work to creep into every aspect of your life. This is an area that we admittedly have not conquered. We are pretty horrible at it. We are praying through this and working through this with you.

One area of working from home that we have succeeded at is creating routines around our work. Our first meeting of the day is quiet time with the Lord. Our second meeting of the day is exercise. After showering, we are ready for our third meeting of the day, breakfast with the family. Building morning consistency creates order and balance throughout the day.

We challenge you to remember that your work should not turn your home into a place of chaos. In the Book of Isaiah chapter 32, after his people have endured military battles with the enemy, the Lord promises them that they will have peaceful dwelling places. Think of modern-day soldiers in the chaos of battle praying for the peace and safety of home, an undisturbed place of rest. How precious these prayers are, especially when we consider that many of us have the privilege of working in our homes in peace. Yet still, we may bring work chaos into our dwelling through lack of discipline.

As we edit this lesson in the wee small hours of the morning, we ask that you pray for us to rein in the chaos of work and be intentional about creating peace in our dwelling places.

Scripture:
My people will live in peaceful dwelling places, in secure homes, in undisturbed places of rest.
Isaiah 32:18

The wise woman builds her house, but with her own hands the foolish one tears hers down.
Proverbs 14:1

Prayer:
Father in Heaven, thank you that even in the great sorrow that has engulfed the world because of the Coronavirus, many businesses have learned that they can get work done from home. I pray for the work that I do at home. Please do not allow it to get out of control. Please help me to keep the hours in check. Please help me keep the physical products of my work tamed so that they are not invading my family space and time.

Call to action:
Take time to write out your weekly work from home schedule. We would love to hear from you. Email us your plan and use the hashtag #PoundCakeHomeSchedule in the subject line.

DAY 16 - KNOW YOUR PARTNER.
TRUST YOUR PARTNER.

We always knew that we would be business partners. We decided to go into business together over 30 years ago before we ever actually knew what the business would be. Each has always been the other's co-conspirator in life's antics. For good or bad, we were raised to be highly functioning co-dependents.

Even before we became business partners, we talked to each other multiple times a day. Do you remember collect calls? In college, we developed what we thought was a genius way to beat the collect call system and communicate on a slim budget.

When the operator would ask, "Will you accept a call from *Thisisdeedeeiloveyou?*" Deana would always decline the charges, but she knew that her big sister was sending her love from Nashville, Tennessee, to Winston-Salem, North Carolina.

Often when there are only two children, they become pigeon-holed into opposites at an early age. Such was the case with us. Perhaps, Dee Dee enthralled a family crowd with a funny or outrageous comment or was noticed dancing as a toddler and automatically became the life of the party. Deana's nearsighted vision gave her glasses at an early age and a studious look to match. Thus, she became labeled a bookworm. These early labels became a self-fulfilling prophecy throughout our adolescent years.

The labels follow us today. We have become so comfortable with these roles that we now embrace them and don't veer from them unless growing the business requires it. If Dee Dee is needed to give a wonky policy-laden presentation, she can and will. If Deana has to act the part of a gregarious social enthusiast, she can and will.

We often joke that if we were one person, we would be superhuman. The reality of business is that you and your partners become one unit. And while you might not be superhuman, you each have superpowers. The mission is advanced when all superpowers are leveraged for the win.

In the lesson, *Hire To Your Weakness*, we go into greater detail about partnering, but for now, we will stress the importance of knowing your partners and trusting your partners. It sounds pretty basic. But you would be surprised at how many people go into business with people they do not like or trust.

Do you trust that your partners are as committed to the mission and vision of the business as you? Disaster awaits you if you neglect this partner-vetting detail. The mission sets the course. All partners must use their superpowers to advance the mission. Advancing the mission has each partner fully aware of the skill sets and attributes of the team. The best partners are eager to let others shine if doing so sets the company up for a mission win. Pursuing a mission win is kryptonite to ego and envy.

When we started in business, Deana saw a query from a Bloomberg Small Business Week reporter. The reporter wanted to interview small business owners about how they relaxed. Deana immediately thought of Dee Dee's time watching cartoons with Dorian. It made a much more colorful pitch than describing her relaxation method of going for a run. Deana submitted the pitch from Dee Dee's point of view. The pitch landed. The reporter interviewed Dee Dee, and we received our first mention in a national magazine. Note Deana's name did not appear anywhere in the interview. However, the win was for the team.

We have seen the green monsters of envy and ego annihilate good businesses. Unfortunately, they often take family relationships and long friendships down in the process.

We are not at all saying you should only partner with people with whom you have an insanely co-dependent relationship. But understand us plainly: life is too important to spend it with people you cannot stand or trust.

Starting and running a business is like starting a family. The hours are grueling. The emotions run high. The funds run low. The odds are against you from day one. So why compound the challenges by partnering with someone you do not fully trust.

The fellowship of believers in the Book Acts is our favorite example of partnership. This is one of the first times the word Christian is used in the Bible. These believers were all dedicated to doing God's work. They broke bread in each other's homes. As you pursue business partners, we encourage you to place trusting them and enjoying their fellowship high on the list of requirements.

Scripture:
They devoted themselves to the apostles' teaching and to fellowship, to the breaking of bread and to prayer.
Acts 2:42

Prayer:
Dear Lord, thank you for the beautiful example of partnership and fellowship in the Book of Acts. Help me model this commitment, honor, and generosity in my relationship with my business partners and family.

Please make me worthy of the trust that I seek in a business partner by being trustworthy myself.

Call to action:
Visit PrayerAndPoundCake.com and take the trustworthy partner challenge.

DAY 17 - HIRE TO YOUR WEAKNESS

Some of the best business advice we ever received came from a mentor and sponsor, Kay Coles James. Mrs. James has held leadership positions in business and government including former director of the U.S. Office of Personnel Management and president of the Heritage Foundation, one of the largest think tanks on the planet. She wisely advised that we hire to our weakness. Human nature makes us more comfortable with people who resemble us in temperament and skill. However, in business, thinking this way leaves you at a disadvantage.

Six years after being in business, we took a long-overdue step. We hired an accountant. As our business has grown, our accounting needs have changed. One fact, however, remains as accurate as it was the day we started. We are not *mathletes*, accountants or tax experts.

We know what we do well, and organizing tax documents and accounting issues is nowhere on the list. If we drafted a list of 1,000 skills we possess, these skills would still not make the cut.

We hired a kind and competent tax preparer in the early days, but she left us to our own devices. If we didn't submit the information that she needed on time or didn't bother to call her at all, she didn't bother to contact us. She was also only $150. If we had any inclination toward being organized in this area, that rate would be a complete steal. But as we are challenged and wretched in this area, $150 ended up being too steep due to the paperwork chaos that we created.

A team full of quarterbacks will not get you to the end zone. You must have a reliable offensive line. This is the exact principle of hiring for diverse skillsets in business. When you hire, or outsource, to your weakness in business, you broaden your skills and expand your areas of expertise.

Scripture:
The way of fools seems right to them, but the wise listen to advice.
Proverbs 12:15

Let the wise listen and add to their learning, and let the discerning get guidance- for understanding proverbs and parables, the sayings and riddles of the wise.
Proverbs 1:5-6

Just as a body, though one, has many parts, but all its many parts form one body, so it is with Christ. For we were all baptized by one Spirit so as to form one body—whether Jews or Gentiles, slave or free—and we were all given the one Spirit to drink. Even so the body is not made up of one part but of many.
1 Corinthians 12:12-14

Prayer:
Father in Heaven, please help me relinquish business areas that are not being served well by my skill set. Give me the humility to understand that every job cannot and should not be fulfilled by me. I pray for existing and future members of my team who will balance out my gifts. I am eager and expectant for their contributions to the business. I know it will lighten my load and improve the offerings of the business.

Call to Action:

Take time today and review the work you are doing for your business. Write down the top five tasks that you perform each day. Then, give an honest evaluation of how you are performing. If your performance is less than A quality, you should strongly consider outsourcing that task and hiring to your weakness.

MIND YOUR BRAND

It takes 20 years to build a reputation and five minutes to ruin it. If you think about that, you'll do things differently.

WARREN BUFFETT

DAY 18 - ELEVATOR PITCH

As a business owner, one of the biggest no-no's is to be stumped when someone asks, "What does your business do?" In theory, this question should be easy to answer. Unfortunately, however, business owners often flub the answer, which is also called an elevator pitch.

Do you have an elevator pitch? You are at a significant disadvantage if you cannot summarize what your business does in under 30 seconds. It's not an elevator pitch to win over funders at a Shark Tank competition. Instead, the elevator pitch is your ability to confidently share what your business does with your friends at a dinner party, moms at a soccer game, or even long-lost college friends over a virtual Zoom reunion.

Your elevator pitch is the verbal front door to your business. How will others ever spread the word if you can't confidently say who you are and what you do?

A lot of people believe their elevator pitch should be a jazzy jingle infomercial narrative. If that is your style, then maybe your elevator pitch should be jazzy and jingly. The most important thing to remember is that the pitch should be authentically you.

Don't be afraid of practicing it over and over again in the mirror and with your close family and friends until you have it honed to perfection.

A close cousin of the "What does your company do?" question is the "Who are your clients?" question. Do not be intimidated by the answer when you don't yet have clients. If you are just starting out, we recommend a pivot by responding in an aspirational way. For example, "ACME Unlimited supports customers who benefit from fill in the blank with your products or services." Of course, when you do have clients, be prepared to rattle them off proudly and boldly.

Christ is the great communicator. He spoke in memorable parables. He also spoke in crisp, clear terms that left little room for misinterpretation about who he is. One such time was in John chapter 14 when he was talking with his disciples. Thomas asks, "Lord, we don't know where you are going, so how can we know the way?"

Jesus' answer is direct and perfect. He says, "I am the way and the truth and the life. No one comes to the Father except through me."

What did he accomplish with these straightforward words? He made it very clear that he alone brings access to the Father. Period. End of discussion.

The salvation of the world is not resting on the clarity of our elevator pitches. But in all things as business owners, it would be wise to model the example of Christ. So, make the description of who you are and what you do clear, confident, and concise.

At Bass Public Affairs, we have two responses to the question, "What do you do?"

Response One: We are a public affairs firm that helps individuals and organizations get in or out of the news.
Response Two: We are the nation's premier public relations firm dedicated to communicating conservative principles to women, millennials, and minority audiences.

In reality, Bass Public Affairs does so much more. But when we have limited time to chat with people, we have discovered that these two quick responses are excellent summaries to explain who we are and invite more opportunities for a deeper discussion about our services.

Scripture:
Jesus answered, "I am the way and the truth and the life. No one comes to the Father except through me. If you really know me, you will know my Father as well. From now on, you do know him and have seen him."
John 14:6-7

Prayer:
Father, you are the greatest communicator. Thank you so much for your word that clearly tells us who you are and how we can be in a relationship with you. You are the way, the truth and the life.

I want to speak with confidence and clarity about my business. So please help me to be deliberate about refining my elevator pitch. Also, please give me more opportunities to share my elevator pitch with friends and perfect strangers.

Call to action:
Share a video of yourself giving your elevator pitch in social media. Tag us using the hashtag #PrayerAndPoundCake.

DAY 19 - CUSTOMER SERVICE IS KING

Customer service is king. You have probably heard the saying, "The customer is always right." Well, we all know the customer is not always right. However, we do believe you should treat the customer as if they are always right. Or, at the very least, you should always treat the customer with the highest level of respect.

Dee Dee has much more experience in direct engagement and customer service, having worked in the restaurant industry and retail from a very young age. In high school, she worked at Pizza Hut and Kirkland's. She even has a brief history as a Mary Kay director. Dee Dee's frontline experiences help craft our customer service policy.

Because Dee Dee has been on the front line directly engaging with customers, she understands intimately that customer service is not something you turn on when you have good customers and dial back when you have customers who are stinkers. Instead, treating customers with kindness and respect should always operate at a gold standard level.

The bottom line is that you are in business for your customers. Yes, you're in business to create a living. You're in business to provide for your family and leave a legacy. But, without your customers, you would not have a business.

We look at two businesses as the gold standard of customer service: Chick-fil-A and Nordstrom.

The Nordstrom shopping experience is peaceful because of subtle actions taken by Nordstrom staff. If you ask Nordstrom sales clerks where to find an item in the store, they rarely point. Instead, they take the time to walk you to the item. Rather than handing you your bag over the counter, they walk around and give it to you. Nordstrom employees win the respect of customers with what is truly above and beyond efforts. The tales of Nordstrom employees who have sorted through dirty vacuum cleaner bags to find a lost diamond ring or raced through Chicago traffic to return left luggage are real.

The Nordstrom employee handbook is based on the principle, "Use your best judgment." The legal responsibilities of the store, of course, require that some things are spelled out. But Nordstrom employees are empowered to resolve confusion with customers by using their best judgment. This philosophy has created a goodwill brand worth its weight in word-of-mouth marketing gold.

Chick-fil-A is the Nordstrom of fast food. If you've ever driven up to a Chick-fil-A window near closing, you have experienced the most pleasant drive-through attendant in town. It doesn't matter where you are in the country. Chick-fil-A service is consistent. They treat you with a high level of kindness and integrity at every one of their establishments. Like Nordstrom, Chick-fil-A's customer service has become as much of a business growth tool as the quality of its product.

Every issue may not be resolved to the customer's desire, but treating the customer with dignity and respect through the process is vital.

We recently saw an example of how not to treat a customer while waiting for our flight to board. A distressed woman at an adjacent gate pleaded with the customer service agent to allow her to board her flight. Unfortunately, the door had closed, the plane was rolling down the tarmac, and boarding was not an option. However, the disrespect that the agent showed the woman made the situation even worse.

As the woman explained that she had a short layover and did her best to race to the gate, the agent noticed a Dunkin Donuts cup in the woman's hand. He said with an experienced level of snark, "Clearly, you had time to get coffee, so you should have had time to make it to your flight." His final comment sent the woman into crying hysterics. He pointed down the long terminal of gates, snarky tone unchanged and said, "I'm sorry, there's nothing I can do for you. You need to go and rebook at the customer service counter."

The agent's assessment was correct. If the woman had time to stop and get a cup of coffee, she certainly had time to make it to her gate before the boarding doors closed. However, the agent's customer service was 100 percent wrong. The airline industry is an easy target for stories about bad customer service. What if for every story of the airline industry getting it wrong, there were a dozen viral stories of a single airline always getting it right? That airline's narrative would be like that of Chick-fil-A's and Nordstrom's. The right thing to do in the situation described here would have been for the agent to remove snark from his tone and show sympathy toward the customer while helping her rebook her flight.

Your customer service strategy should not be accidental. Instead, your plan should be a deliberate map of the way you want customers to feel from their first encounter with your business to the time the sale is final and beyond.

Scripture:
A gentle answer turns away wrath, but a harsh word stirs up anger.
Proverbs 15:1

For they refreshed my spirit and yours also. So men deserve recognition.
1 Corinthians 16:18

Prayer:
Dear Lord, I want my business to be as widely known for how we treat our customers as it is known for the high-quality products and services that we offer. Therefore, in every single interaction with customers, may every single word be gentle, uplifting and respectful.

I commit to celebrating with my customers regularly. I also commit to recognizing and celebrating the excellent work of my employees and consultants.

Please, Lord, allow me to always put myself in the other person's shoes. Help me to treat others the way I want to be treated. I pray, dear Lord, that your light shines through me every day in all my interactions—personal and professional. I know that a small act of kindness can change the trajectory of someone's day or even their life.

Call to action:
The next time you receive outstanding customer service, ask to speak with the manager and give a shout-out and words of praise.

DAY 20 - LIVE LIFE ON THE RECORD

In our business, we deal with reporters on an almost daily basis. When speaking to journalists, friends, colleagues or foe, you should understand a few key terms. They are "on the record," "on background," and "off the record."

On the record, of course, means whatever you say may be used in a news story and attributed to you. On background means that the information can be used but not attributed to you. Off the record means that what you are saying is not for reporting at all.

We believe in living a life and conducting business that is always on the record. This practice served Deana well when she met Dr. Ben Carson to interview for the role of press secretary on his 2016 presidential campaign. Jim Rutenberg accurately reported that Deana was "momentarily speechless" to discover that a *New York Times* reporter would be sitting in on her interview. But every word that she uttered, she would have said whether for public or private distribution.

In this age of cell phone videos and mini audio recording devices, every word you utter has the potential to be on the record. Even if you are dealing with a journalist who agrees that the conversation is off the record, we advise that it is best to assume every single thing you say may end up in print or on the air. If you live life on the record, you won't be shocked if your words appear in the press. If politicians governed themselves by this principle, we would have fewer hot mic embarrassments.

In one of Bob Hope's classic screwball comedies, *Nothing But the Truth*, his character makes a bet that he can go without lying for a full day and still succeed in business. Most of his subsequent truth-telling comes in the form of hurtful insults, producing comedic chaos.

For us, living life on the record does not mean speaking every raw, painful truth walking around in our brains. Instead, living life on the record means that you censor harsh and unkind words, even if true.

We host a weekly podcast called *Policy and Pound Cake*. The rallying cry and social media hashtag of the podcast is #AttackPolicyNotPeople. We believe this plan of attacking policy and not people is the best way to approach life and business. Whether in conflict with a partner, customer or vendor, living life on the record works best when we leave personal attacks out of the conversation and focus on policies. By attacking policies and not people, we have a better chance of reaching a harmonious resolution.

Scripture:
May these words of my mouth and this meditation of my heart be pleasing in your sight, Lord, my Rock and my Redeemer.
Psalm 19:14

The soothing tongue is a tree of life, but a perverse tongue crushes the spirit.
Proverbs 15:4

Prayer:
Dear Lord, I don't want to live a double life, speaking one way in public and another in private. So please help me to live a life on the record, always sharing messages that will honor you. Please let my words be words that will build up

people and not tear them down. I pray that my words draw people to you and not push people from you. Please bind my tongue and confuse my language if my words bring you dishonor.

Call to action:
Today's call to action focuses on self-reflection. Assess the way you talk to your friends and family and the way you speak to your staff. If you would not want your manner to be made public, take immediate action to course correct.

DAY 21 - NEVER LET THEM SEE YOU SWEAT

One of our favorite commercials from the '80s is a Dry Idea deodorant ad starring actor Robert Woods from *One Life to Live* and *All My Children*. He says, "There are three *nevers* in Hollywood. Never pick up the phone on the first ring. Never say I'll be right over. And never, I don't care how much you want the part, never let them see you sweat. It's okay to be anxious, as long as you don't look anxious."

You might be anxious, but you must not behave in an anxious manner. You might get nervous. You will possibly even fill unhinged, but the reality is that you don't have to be! God has got your back in every situation before every adversary. So, you do not have to look or behave as if you're unhinged.

Deana's first real job was working as an admissions counselor for her alma mater Salem College in Winston-Salem, North Carolina. At this job, Deana received wise advice from her boss Katherine Knapp Watts. When a co-worker could not attend a college fair 30 minutes away in Greensboro, Katherine asked Deana to step in to manage Salem's booth. The college fair was a huge event and in one of Salem's key recruiting markets. By the time Deana left the office, the fair would already be in full swing. As Deana frantically threw recruitment supplies into the travel case, Katherine stopped her. She said, "You are already late. You will walk in late. There is nothing you can do about it now. So, walk in calmly as if everything is under control and according to plan."

What a powerful and important lesson for life. Just because plans go sideways does not mean you have to lose control. The way you respond when the chaos erupts can improve your business or destroy it. Your employees and your partners are looking to you, and you must behave like a leader.

The poster child for never letting them see you sweat is our sweet mama. Raised in a tiny town in Georgia on a red dirt road, she began life with little more than the love and adoration of her mother and father and the assurance of God's grace. That was more than enough to give her the courage to tackle any challenge that comes her way. Through death and sickness and financial devastation, we have seen her stand, unshakable as a magnolia, providing comfort and shade for generations of our family. There is no political leader or business tycoon to whom she would bow in subservience.

We are forever grateful that our mama taught us early in life that being anxious usually comes from focusing on other people _ what they think or what they will do. When focused on yourself and the task at hand, there is little time and no need to stress over the actions of others. Our mama often says to us, "How dare you be terrified of regular human beings? They put their pants on one leg at a time, just like you."

Scripture:
Get yourself ready! Stand up and say to them whatever I command you. Do not be terrified by them, or I will terrify you before them.
Jeremiah 1:17

I have told you these things, so that in me you may have peace. In this world you will have trouble. But take heart! I have overcome the world.
John 16:33

Prayer:

My amazing God, I have nothing to fear because you are with me always. I know in each business and personal interaction, you have stood by me, Lord. I will not be terrified or intimidated by any encounter with people on Earth. They are mere mortals, and I am your child, a co-heir with Christ. Please let me remember who I am and take away any anxiety.

Lord, I lean on you because I know you are my help and my protector. I have given my life and my will over to you, and in doing so, I have power, Lord, to be strong and not afraid.

Call to action:

Make a list of the people and situations that bring you anxiety. Think of the very worst thing that could happen if everything goes wrong. Review each item and ask: "Is this able to separate me from God's love and grace?" If the answer is "No," draw a thick, black line through that item. At the end of this exercise, your list should now look like a highly redacted top-secret document. Every single item should have a black line. Nothing can separate you from God's love and grace.

DAY 22 - PULLING A FALLON CARRINGTON

When we were girls growing up in Georgia, one of our pastimes was watching shows like *Dallas*, *Dynasty*, and *Knots Landing*. It was an escape from our ordinary, working-class existence. Like millions of Americans, we tuned in to see who shot J.R. and to see the sequin-costumed catfights between Joan Collins and Linda Evans.

In season one, episode four of *Dynasty*, Crystal Carrington has married the wealthy oil tycoon Blake Carrington. Crystal has a bit of adjusting to do because she does not come from the world of oil fields and private jets. In this episode, Crystal's stepdaughter, Fallon, tries to school her stepmother in the ways of the rich.

Blake Carrington is hosting a huge dinner for the most prominent of his fellow tycoons. They are not yet aware that Blake is having a financial crisis. Because of the financial drought, Crystal is confused when a fashion designer arrives to help her select her wardrobe for the event and for the season. The average cost for such a wardrobe, she is told, is about $150,000.

This episode aired in 1981. That would be equivalent to about $280,000 today. Could you imagine spending a fraction of that amount on your seasonal wardrobe when your company is on the brink of ruin? Well, because financial ruin is on the horizon, Crystal sensibly sends the man away.

She feels like the family needs to tighten its belt. At this point, Fallon begins to educate Crystal on how the rich do it.

Fallon tells Crystal that she has to have a new wardrobe because if the wealthy oil tycoons and their wives see Crystal in last season's clothes, they will know that Blake is in dire financial straits. They will see blood in the water.

Crystal, thankful for the advice, does not want to embarrass her husband. She calls the fashion buyer back and orders the appropriate clothes to look like a billionaire's wife. Some people call this "faking it till you make it." For decades, in our family, we called this pulling a Fallon.

Without anything like the Carringtons' bank account, we have "pulled Fallons" of our own. Before Dee Dee's first day of work at MBNA in Wilmington, Delaware, Mama treated her on a trip to Casual Corners. She had her Sunday best, but we reasoned that she needed something more for her first day in corporate America.

Some people fake it until they make it right into more debt. Therefore, in the 40 years since that episode aired and the 20 years since Dee Dee's first day at MBNA, we have fine-tuned our definition of "pulling a Fallon." Our fine-tuned version of pulling a Fallon is making sound decisions about investments to build your brand. It's not as catchy, but you get our point. There will be times when you need to buy that power suit or invest in that software, even when the coffers are low. That is very different from faking it until you make it. Pulling a Fallon does not mean buying the latest Ferragamo or Goyard item to impress your peers who have no ability to or intention of bringing you any business.

Pulling a Fallon is strategic spending, not unnecessary debt and extravagance. Learn this lesson or face the consequences.

You do not have to navigate the journey to financial literacy alone. There are fantastic resources and organizations to guide you. Dee Dee serves on the board of directors for the national non-profit Smart Women Smart Money. We are champions of Smart Women Smart Money because it empowers women from all walks of life to lean into and take control of their financial destiny. Through workshops and retreats, we have seen women embrace their motto that it is *never too early and never too late.*

Scripture:
One person pretends to be rich, yet has nothing; another pretends to be poor, yet has great wealth.
Proverbs 13:7

Prayer:
Dear Lord, I don't want to get caught up in the trap of financially overextending myself to pretend to have the trappings of a successful business. I want to build a successful business through sound financial principles.

Please let the way I manage my personal and business finances be a witness and a blessing to my family and business partners.

Call to action:
Take a look at your business expenses for the last quarter. Were the purchases sound and necessary for operating your business? If you have a long list of items that would fall under faking it until you make it, we advise you to extend the call to action and review your business expenses for the last year.

Visit PrayerAndPoundCake.com for resources to empower and train you.

DAY 23 - LIVE LIFE UNOFFENDED

One of the best pieces of advice we have received over the years came from a dear friend, Anne Bennett. It is simple. Live life unoffended. If we go around taking offense at every slight or perceived slight, we will live in pure misery.

People have the capacity to be offended by almost anything in this world. Some are offended if they are not greeted when they enter a room or if their name is omitted from a program. We have seen colleagues completely unable to enjoy an event when they felt slighted by their seating in the table hierarchy.

It is easier to live an unoffended life by remembering that most of the time, people do not realize they are offending you. They are not intentionally trying to harm you or hurt you. Usually, they are not even thinking about you.

That being said, our offense is often more a product of our own arrogance and insecurity than any action taken by the person who supposedly offended us. But, for the sake of argument, let's say they actually behaved or spoke in an intentionally offensive way. If you let it eat away at you, clouding your mood and perhaps even moving you to retaliate in kind, you may create more problems for yourself and, more importantly, dishonor God.

There may be legitimate reasons for you to be offended when people are seriously trying to undermine you and belittle you. This is not a call to be a doormat. It is a call to govern your responses in a way that would allow you to have joy and not gloom and despair.

When you know your value, you are less likely to be offended by others. One very earthly example of this played out when we were staffing Dr. Carson for an event in New York. We rose early to meet our friend, mentor, and sponsor Armstrong Williams at the hotel's Kinkos to print a final copy of Dr. Carson's remarks. We shared our print order with the Kinko's clerk. He said one of his two machines was down, and it would take a few minutes to get the second one up and running. With the order placed, the clerk went to the back room, and we sat in chairs near the entrance and waited patiently.

Within minutes, a tall stylish blond walked in and asked us if we were open and if we could help her fax a document. She didn't ask if the *store* was open. She asked if we were open. She did not ask if we could get a Kinko's clerk to help her fax a document because she thought we were the clerks. This is not the first time we were mistaken for "the help." It usually offends us. But we watched Armstrong. Before we could shame her with her assumptions that we worked at Kinkos, Armstrong stood and began to help her at the self-serve fax station as if he were a long-serving Kinko's employee.

A mega-multimillionaire, owner of a dozen television stations, and real estate interests around the globe, Armstrong was more amused than offended. He was amused because he knew his value, and the woman's assumptions had no bearing on who he is.

Scripture:
Fools show their annoyance at once, but the prudent overlook an insult.
Proverbs 12:16

A person's wisdom yields patience; it is to one's glory to overlook an offense.
Proverbs 19:11

Prayer:
Dear Lord, I want others to see me anticipating the good in everyone.

Help me to be humble and not take every slight as an assault on my character and reputation. Allow me to extend grace when I feel slighted. I want to use every perceived offense as an opportunity to pray for those who may have offended me. Especially if the slight was intended, allow me to forgive them and pray for them.

Call to action:
Take a moment to think of the last person who offended you and pray for them.

CHRIST CENTRIC BUSINESS

I believe in Christianity as I believe that the Sun has risen, not only because I see it but because by it, I see everything else.

C.S. LEWIS

DAY 24 - FIRST THINGS FIRST

One of the most challenging things to do in running your own business is managing your time. There are a thousand things in a single day that may appear to be a priority. Notice we said, appear to be a priority. Really, on any given day, there are about two to three legitimate priorities. So those are the tasks that you should tackle first. Because the things that we measure or track, we are more likely to do, we encourage you to make prayer and praise a priority. Add it to your task list.

It is essential to have a list of goals and accomplishments. But your daily task list must be realistic. One of the issues that we continue to struggle with is attempting to tackle all of those goals in a single day. Having a system that allows you to chip away at tangible goals every day gives you a sense of accomplishment and a sense of being a true finisher. If you allow yourself to put too many tasks on a daily to-do list and realistically, you have the time only to accomplish two of those tasks, you ultimately begin to feel defeated. So, when we approach our daily to-do list, we do so by applying the principle of first things first. What is the first and most important thing that must be accomplished? Do that first. Mark Twain called this "eating your frogs."

We even set our alarm clock for 12:34 p.m. to remind us to be in order, one, two, three, four. It's a time in the middle of the day to ask the question, are we putting the first things first? Only you can know what that first thing should be. Is it a client presentation due the next morning, or is it prepping for a conference call that is moments away?

There are many tools and apps to help you get organized with your first things first task list. In our experience, we have found that the more bells and whistles, the less likely we are to use them. We are very old-fashioned. We keep our daily tasks in our canvas journals.

We also keep a master content and editorial calendar that forecasts long-term tasks, events, and programs for the entire year. To track long-term tasks and goals, we use Google Docs and sheets for ease of use while in collaboration. Victoria and Whitney, two of our interns, introduced us to Google products years ago, and we have not looked back. For some of you, Google may not be sophisticated enough. For others, it may be too sophisticated. You have to find the system that works for you.

The items on the long-term calendar are important. However, we must tackle the first things first.

Scripture:
But seek first His kingdom and His righteousness, and all these things will be given to you as well.
Matthew 6:33

Prayer:
Heavenly Father, your words are clear; seek you first. In the busyness of starting my business Lord, help me to keep my priorities in order. I want to stop and thank you first in all things, big and small. I want to start each day with my face toward you, Lord hearing your words for me, receiving your directions, and being obedient.

For me, the first thing must be putting you in the place of honor and priority in my work and professional life.

Call to action:
Review your task list and determine what priorities are for tomorrow. The list cannot include more than three tasks.

DAY 25 - SHERYL SANDBERG'S HUSBAND HAS DIED

If you want to watch grown people behave badly, we recommend you participate in a presidential campaign. These campaigns are the Super Bowl of politics. You are swimming with the sharks of political strategists and operatives. Even a candidate as honest, decent and kind as Dr. Ben Carson inevitably hires operatives accustomed to the swamp of politics. Anything but cutthroat, swamp operatives Bass Public Affairs was honored to be selected to work for Dr. Carson's campaign.

As Deana prepared to make her way to Detroit for Dr. Carson's official campaign announcement, one petty campaign intrigue after another had her furious.

On her way to the airport, fuming over some insignificant test of her patience, she received a media alert on her iPhone. Sheryl Sandburg's husband, Dave Goldberg, was dead.

We count ourselves among the many women encouraged by Sandberg's remarkable career and her wise counsel to lean in. On that day, as Deana fumed over the small and the petty, Sheryl Sandberg was struggling with the real and worthy.

Sheryl Sandberg, one of the most powerful names in big tech and business, had been reduced to a regular mortal. Her beloved had died. That news alert gave Deana pause. It jolted her back to the things that matter. It reminded her that all of the campaign shenanigans were irrelevant. The things that mattered were her cheerleaders and her champions.

Dee Dee consistently teaches her kids lessons that must transfer into the way we do business. Each morning during carpool drop-off when Dee Dee's babies were in elementary school, she said to them, "Be a good listener, be a good student and be a good friend." It sounds so basic, but the underlining theme is to *be good*. We know in our hearts that we are not operating in a good place when life is filled with malicious gossip and petty fights. You know from your own lived experience that you operate at a higher, more effective level, when you are not focused on petty victories.

Scripture:
Finally, brothers and sisters, whatever is true, whatever is noble, whatever is right, whatever is pure, whatever is lovely, whatever is admirable—if anything is excellent or praiseworthy—think about such things.
Philippians 4:8

Prayer:
Most merciful Father, I come to today asking that you show me how to keep things in perspective. Please help me to keep my priorities in order. I know that my troubles, great and small, are on your radar. Please, Lord, let me distinguish between issues that are great and insignificant petty matters. You will never leave me to face my challenges alone, no matter what they are. For this Lord, I am grateful. Thank you for your mercy.

Call to action:
Eliminate the petty things in life.

DAY 26 - LAUGHTER IS NECESSARY

We have included a lesson on laughter because laughter gives us the energy to continue when days are long and work is hard. Breaking out into hysterical laughter for no reason lightens our load.

We also believe healthy laughter can be used as a barometer to measure the health of other aspects of your business.

Does your relationship with your business partner give you room for laughter? We don't mean fake polite laughter. But can you break out into uncontrollable tears and snot laughter? You likely spend most of your waking hours with your business partners. If the time you spend with your business partners is all serious and void of laughter, we believe that it affects your business success. It certainly affects your joy.

According to The Mayo Clinic, laughter stimulates your heart, lungs and muscles. Laughter relieves stress, soothes tension and improves your immune system. Studies confirm that laughing, the ability to laugh out loud, is actually as important as eating right and sleeping. So, we encourage laughter as a health measure for your personal and professional well-being.

We are blessed to have a relationship that generates spontaneous, ridiculous laughter all the time and anytime. However, if you have to begin by building in comedy breaks, we say, do it! Take a break, go to YouTube, and watch something silly that has absolutely nothing to do with work.

We trust the science that confirms laughter is healthy, and by that, we mean that laughter improves your physical health. But we also believe that laughter improves your mental health. If you can laugh at situations and move beyond the situation, you are less likely to allow negative seeds to take root and grow. Laughing at life and work mishaps shows your ability to put all of this work in perspective.

If you have ever listened to our weekly podcast, *Policy and Pound Cake*, it is clear that our relationship is born of laughter. We have been laughing together for almost five decades. We also recognize that when we laugh, the energy, the spirit, the attitude, the tension around us is lightened.

Today, we want you to understand that having a deliberate plan, an intentional laughter and joy strategy is essential. This is not only important for you and your partners, but it is also important for your clients and your employees. When you lead with laughter, it spills over to those on your team.

Scripture:

All the days of the oppressed are wretched, but the cheerful heart has a continual feast.
Proverbs 15:15

A cheerful heart is good medicine, but a crushed spirit dries up the bones.
Proverbs 17:22

She is clothed with strength and dignity; she can laugh at the days to come.
Proverbs 31:25

Prayer:

Dear Lord, thank you for creating laughter. Help me lighten my load and lighten my team's load by being willing to laugh at myself and enjoy good humor.

Would you please help me to have a cheerful heart and be good medicine to those with crushed spirits around me?

Call to action:

Take a break and find your own laugh track. Seriously. No joke! If you need prompts, visit the laugh track in the resources offered at PrayerAndPoundCake.com.

DAY 27 - REMEMBER WHOSE YOU ARE

In running a business, you will have days when you feel overwhelmed and completely outdone by circumstances. You may even want to call it quits, but we encourage you to remember whose you are and to remember what you've endured. Remember what it took to get you here.

One of our favorite stories in the Bible is the story of Jesse's son, a poor shepherd boy who defeated Goliath with five smooth stones and a sling shot. David defeated Goliath *because* he was a poor shepherd boy not *in spite of being* a poor shepherd boy. Goliath was expecting David to fight on his terms, wearing his clunky armor. But David said, "Nope." He knew Goliath would clobber him if he tried to fight him in the traditional way. So, David used unconventional warfare, and the rest is God's history.

Those of us who come from what may appear to be humble beginnings often feel at a disadvantage because we were not born with the tools of business. David's slingshot verses Goliath's armor should be enough to teach us that our tools are good enough. It's those humble, rough, and scrabble beginnings that give us the grit to make our dreams turn into reality.

We have to look at the stock from which we are born. We are descendants of brave men and women who survived the middle passage. If they could survive the middle passage, we can survive the tough days we are experiencing. If they can endure the middle passage, you can survive the next contentious board meeting. You can survive the next product launch. You can survive the next item on your task list.

When you remember who you are, it will help govern your decisions in challenging situations. You will not bend to the whims of people advising you to make wrong or immoral decisions. You don't want to betray or ruin a legacy that has been left to you.

When we started our business, we invested in a ridiculous phone system with buttons to press to reach various departments. The goal was to make our firm sound like behemoth powerhouse. But we soon realized that our secret sauce was the fact that we are a small shop with a personal touch that you will never get from a giant firm. Our mama makes our clients her homemade pound cake. Homemade pound cake is who we are. It is our edge. What is yours?

Scripture:
Then Saul dressed David in his own tunic. He put a coat of armor on him and a bronze helmet on his head. David fastened on his sword over the tunic and tried walking around, because he was not used to them.

"I cannot go in these," he said to Saul, "because I am not used to them." So he took them off. Then he took his staff in his hand, chose five smooth stones from the stream, put them in the pouch of his shepherd's bag and, with his sling in his hand, approached the Philistine.
1 Samuel 17:38-40

Prayer:
Dear Lord, thank you for my rich history. Thank you for ancestors known and unknown who survived during times

far more dangerous and primitive than those that I face. Thank you even more that I am a co-heir with Christ. My earthly lineage gives me courage. My heavenly lineage completely fortifies my soul and steadies my heart to not give up.

Call To Action:
Learn the story of one of your ancestors who survived and thrived during circumstances more challenging than your own.

DAY 28 - EQUALLY YOKED IN BUSINESS

What does it mean to be unequally yoked in business? We often hear that phrase when talking about personal, romantic relationships, but what does it mean to be yoked equally to your business significant other?

Well, let us tell you what it does not mean. It does not mean that your business partner should be exactly like you. It does not mean your business partner must dress like you, act like you, talk like you, or have the same Myers-Briggs personality test results that you have. As we discussed in *Hire To Your Weakness*, it's clear that having different skill sets is a valuable and, in many cases, a critical component of being in partnership with someone.

When it comes to being unequally yoked in your business, we mean that you and your business partners share a different vision and a different mission for the business.

First of all, if you don't have a clearly defined vision or mission, you may not even realize that you are unequally yoked. You could be operating under one vision, and your business partners could be operating under a different vision. Your company could be moving right along until the divergent visions begin to tear the business apart. So being equally yoked means being of like mind in the vision and the mission of your business.

If you have not signed on the dotted line and are not yet official business partners, it is vital that you agree with the mission and vision of your business before you enter into a legal partnership. Do not assume that you are on the same page. Talk it out. Spell it out. Make it clear.

If you are already in business and discover you are not of one mind on the mission of the business, we are in no way saying call it quits and dissolve the partnership. But agreeing on the direction of the business, both short-term and long-term goals, is necessary.

We are of one mine on the overall mission and vision of our business. However, along the way, we discover that we may not be on the same page about various projects. As soon as that discovery is made, we have to talk it out and course correct. In most cases, it requires one or both of us to make compromises. But the compromise is always a win because it puts us walking toward the same goal.

Scripture:
Do not be yoked together with unbelievers. For what do righteousness and wickedness have in common? Or what fellowship can light have with darkness?
2 Corinthians 6:14

Prayer:
Dear Lord, help me be wise about entering into a business partnership. Direct me to partners you believe want the best for this business as I do. When those moments come when we may not see eye to eye, allow us to seek your face Lord, setting differences aside and do what is financially and morally right for the business.

Call To Action:
Visit PrayerAndPoundCake.com and take the five-minute business partner challenge with your business partner. Discover how you both answer mission and vision questions about your business.

DAY 29 - YOUR TRIBE

One of our favorite books of the Bible is Acts. The phrase Christian is only used three times in the New Testament. Two of those times are in Acts (Acts 11:26, Acts 26:28). Earlier in Acts chapter two, we are given a description of true fellowship.

The believers in Acts are devoted to each other through their devotion to God. They shared everything. They ate together, worshipped together, served the poor together. They were strengthened by each other. If you believe you can do this life alone, you are wrong. If you do not have a fellowship of believers, you need them. God built you to be in fellowship.

Saying that you should have close friends seems so elementary. However, we have included this lesson because so many people get friendship wrong. In a true tribe, iron sharpens iron. You must actively support others. Don't be the person who always asks people to support your endeavors but disappears when it comes to helping others. Offer and seek support.

We are blessed with our small fellowship of believers. Our incredible intimate tribe of friends and family loves the Lord. Their devotion to us and enthusiasm for us are born from their love of Christ. Whether it is giving a like to a post on social media or attending events to help us beef up the crowd or stopping in the middle of their day to pray with us, our tribe wants us to win.

Do you have prayer warriors in your tribe? If you are going to war, you need your own prayer seal team. Our prayer seal team is a diverse group of women who are not playing when it comes to their faith in Jesus. They are honest brokers for Jesus and they are unwilling to co-sign our disfunction if it dishonors Christ. We call them our own personal JSOC – Jesus Special Operations Command. When stuff is going down in this world, your JSOC has your six. If we picked up the phone and called Lanie Ehlinger, Pat Ware, L'Tanya Brown, Whitney Rhodes, Jennifer Wilson or Tanisha Watson right now and said we need to pray, they would say, "Let's Do It!"

When we tell them of our victories, they are singing hallelujah praises with us. We call them for wise counsel. Their reverence for God will not allow them to blow smoke up our behinds. If we are wrong, they say so. They give us sincere praise and fair criticism because they want what's best for us. They are sharpening us to be used by God.

Amani Council, one member of our tribe posted this on social media. "If you don't get excited seeing your friends win, you are weird and should probably stay away from me." We could not agree more.

Your tribe does not necessarily include your business partner, co-workers, mentors, sponsors or even your biological family. The platinum cardmembers of our tribe love us as unconditionally as humanly possible. No roadblock stands in the way of them wanting us to do well.

We are blessed to have tribes from all seasons of our life. Dee Dee has a tribe of Delta Sigma Theta Sorority sisters, Jack and Jill of America moms and Fisk University alumni. Deana has a tribe of Salem College sisters, Bible study buddies and Alexandria Strategy Group champions. We have nurtured relationships along the way that have produced clusters of supporters who will celebrate every success we achieve.

Our core tribe, our innermost circle, happens to be our family. We even have a family name, *The Wild Bunch.* Not one member of The Wild Bunch will ever feel or be alone if the rest of us are on this planet. Having this unconditional gang of champions in our corner sharpens us to keep going. Every member of The Wild Bunch puts in the work to celebrate and support each other.

Why is this lesson necessary in a book about business success? Building a true tribe is necessary because human relationships are *the thing.* The love and respect of real people are all we have left in the end. If you don't have this in your life, we want it for you so desperately because we know how life-giving our tribe has been to us. Build your tribe.

Scripture:
As iron sharpens iron, so one person sharpens another.
Proverbs 27:17

They devoted themselves to the apostles' teaching and fellowship, to the breaking of bread and to prayer. Everyone was filled with awe at the many wonders and signs performed by the apostles. All the believers were together and had everything in common. They sold property and possessions to give to anyone who had need. Every day they continued to meet together in the temple courts. They broke bread in their homes and ate together with glad and sincere hearts, praising God and enjoying the favor of all the people. And the Lord added to their number daily those who were being saved.
Acts 2: 42-47

Prayer:
Dear Lord, thank you for your example in the Book of Acts about the fellowship of believers. Thank you for the people in my life who have had my back and supported me. Help

me to be intentional about building and fortifying my tribe. I pray for discernment about who should be in my inner circle. Give me clear opportunities to show my unconditional love and support for my tribe.

Lord, I pray for a tribe that would love and support me unconditionally. I pray for a tribe of people who know you, and because of their knowledge of you, they show grace and mercy to me.

Let be to others what you have been to me, a refuge and comfort.

Call To Action:
We invite you to join our virtual tribe by visiting PrayerAndPoundCake.com. But you must build a real-life in-person human connection tribe. If you do not have a true ride-or-die tribe, there is no better time than this moment to begin doing the work. It may be awkward, but it is necessary. Pray about the people who should be in your inner circle.

DAY 30 - SLEEP IS NOT OVERRATED

Today, we offer sound advice that we are not consistently following. Sleep is not overrated. God designed our bodies to work and rest. We could cite report after report confirming the importance of sleep. But you are the proof. You know the necessity of sleep based on your lived experiences.

We are both married to highly accomplished men who require eight hours of sleep. For years, we bragged about our ability to function on four hours of sleep or less. Today, we acknowledge that under sleeping for four hours and merely "functioning" is not as impressive as sleeping for eight hours and killing it.

We must confess that our tendency to work into the wee, morning hours reveals our failings at time management and our lack of trust in God. Even though we have kidded ourselves by saying it showed that we had true grit and a strong work ethic.

The hard truth is if we prioritized, delegated, and set realistic workday goals, two o'clock in the morning work sessions would not be necessary. Perhaps it's time for us to revisit the lessons from *Hire to Your Weakness* and *First Things First*. Think about the tasks that have you missing sleep. Are they life-or-death critical to your business? Ninety percent of the time, they are not.

Running on little sleep screams a lack of trust in God because it shows an unwillingness to be still and trust that God will not forsake you.

For us, the law of diminishing returns comes into play after a certain number of uninterrupted work hours. The quality of our work suffers as the quality of our work product is reduced.

Scripture:
He says, "Be still, and know that I am God; I will be exalted among the nations, I will be exalted in the earth."
Psalm 46:10

Because of the Lord's great love we are not consumed, for his compassions never fail. They are new every morning; great is your faithfulness.
Lamentations 3:22-23

Prayer:
Heavenly Father, I want to rest and recover. So please help me to place a priority on sleep. I don't want to be sidelined because of my inability to manage my time. I don't want to be sidelined because of my fear and restlessness. I want to be still and know that you are God. I want to seek and hear your voice in the stillness. I want to be refreshed each morning by your compassion for me.

I sit in awe of you, Dear God. You created time, and you celebrate rest.

Call To Action:
Be still for ten minutes. Don't think about work. Just be still. Tonight, go to sleep.

DAY 31 - KEEP PRAYING

We end our 31 days where we should begin every single day, offering praises to God. We offer praises that there are no barriers between God and us. What crazy awesome news!! We do not need a middleman. We have the freedom to call on the CEO of the universe. He has an open-door policy. That door is opened through prayer.

So, keep praying. In our experience, some of the most amazing blessings and moments of clarity come when we are making the conscious choice to be disciplined in prayer.

In the Book of Genesis, Abraham sent his servant to find a wife for Isaac, and while the servant was praying for a woman exactly like Rebekah, Rebekah showed up. In the Book of Acts, Peter's friends were praying for Peter to be freed from prison, and when he knocked on the door to interrupt their prayer time, they were astonished.

Scripture:

Then he prayed, "Lord, God of my master Abraham, make me successful today, and show kindness to my master Abraham. See, I am standing beside this spring, and the daughters of the townspeople are coming out to draw water. May it be that when I say to a young woman, 'Please let down your jar that I may have a drink,' and she says, 'Drink, and I'll water your camels too'—let her be the one you have chosen for your servant Isaac. By this I will know that you have shown kindness to my master." Before he had finished praying, Rebekah came out with her jar on her shoulder. Genesis 24:12-15

Then the angel said to him, "Put on your clothes and sandals." And Peter did so. "Wrap your cloak around you and follow me," the angel told him. Peter followed him out of the prison, but he had no idea that what the angel was doing was really happening; he thought he was seeing a vision. They passed the first and second guards and came to the iron gate leading to the city. It opened for them by itself, and they went through it. When they had walked the length of one street, suddenly the angel left him.

Then Peter came to himself and said, "Now I know without a doubt that the Lord has sent his angel and rescued me from Herod's clutches and from everything the Jewish people were hoping would happen."

When this had dawned on him, he went to the house of Mary the mother of John, also called Mark, where many people had gathered and were praying. Peter knocked at the outer entrance, and a servant named Rhoda came to answer the door. When she recognized Peter's voice, she was so overjoyed she ran back without opening it and exclaimed, "Peter is at the door!"

"You're out of your mind," they told her. When she kept insisting that it was so, they said, "It must be his angel." Acts: 12:8-16

Our Prayer for You:
Dear Lord, thank you for a tribe of readers and entrepreneurs who are willing to pray for your guidance and blessings over their business.

We pray that you multiply the success of each readers' business and that every single day they give you the glory.

God, we know that you live in the praises of your people. We praise you forever and ever, amen.

Our Call To Action:
We will keep praying for you.

We are each other's harvest; we are each other's business; we are each other's magnitude and bond.
Gwendolyn Brooks

THE BONDGIRL BOOKS STORY

Shortly before the Civil War, a mixed-race slave girl escaped her North Carolina captors by donning men's clothing and fleeing to New York through the Underground Railroad. The fictionalized, autobiographical account of her life as a fugitive slave is told in *The Bondwoman's Narrative*. She uses the pen name Hannah Crafts to write the narrative. However, thanks to the research of historians Henry Louis Gates, Jr., and Gregg Hecimovich, the true author of the manuscript is revealed to be Hannah Bond.

Hannah Bond knew that learning to read was punishable by death. Fear of death did not stop her from taking her first flight to freedom by learning to read and write.

Her second flight to freedom is told in *The Bondwoman's Narrative* written in the mid-1850s. The work is the only known book written by a fugitive slave woman and most likely the first novel ever written by an African-American woman.

Today, BondGirl Books stands on the shoulders of Hannah Bond.

BondGirl Books is an independent publishing house and community of readers who meet online and in real life to share the love of reading. To join our community visit BondGirlBooks.com.

Made in the USA
Middletown, DE
16 February 2022